Varnished
Without A Trace

Also by Misty Simon

Carpet Diem
Deceased and Desist
Grounds for Remorse
Cremains of the Day

Varnished Without A Trace

A Tallie Graver Mystery

Misty Simon

KENSINGTON BOOKS
www.kensingtonbooks.com

KENSINGTON BOOKS are published by

Kensington Publishing Corp.
119 West 40th Street
New York, NY 10018

All Kensington titles, imprints, and distributed lines are available at special quantity discounts for bulk purchases for sales promotion, premiums, fund-raising, educational, or institutional use.

Special book excerpts or customized printings can also be created to fit specific needs. For details, write or phone the office of the Kensington Sales Manager: Attn.: Sales Department. Kensington Publishing Corp., 119 West 40th Street, New York, NY 10018. Phone: 1-800-221-2647.

Kensington and the K logo Reg. U.S. Pat. & TM Off.

First Printing: October 2020
ISBN-13: 978-1-4967-2376-5
ISBN-10: 1-4967-2376-7

ISBN-13: 978-1-4967-2377-2 (ebook)
ISBN-10: 1-4967-2377-5 (ebook)

10 9 8 7 6 5 4 3 2 1

Printed in the United States of America

To Daniel who makes me laugh and holds my
hand and my heart

Chapter One

Here in central Pennsylvania, bingo could very easily be considered a death sport, filled with hurled insults, hurled troll dolls and the occasional hurled beer bottle, depending on the venue. It could be nasty and cutthroat. And that was just in the first hour.

Maybe in other parts of the world it was a happy, fun game, with joyous shouts of winning and prizes galore, from money to baskets. Maybe people gathered together with dried corn and game cards that had seen a lot of use over the years, a lot of laughs and a lot of woo-hooing.

We, however, had a medic on hand in case things got, well, out of hand. Like that one time a bingo caller, the guy who pulled the numbers and read them off, was given a fat lip after the last game. No caller had yet landed in my family's funeral home due to grievous injuries from doing their volunteer job, but I wouldn't have been too surprised if that ever happened.

In my town, though, as in others in our state, it was kill-or-be-killed regarding a game dependent solely on a cage full of balls and some cards with corresponding numbers. Even if it was Christmas Eve.

I just hoped the rash of fires we'd had recently wouldn't interrupt the game. Then again, maybe that was exactly what was needed tonight to get me out of what could be an awful evening. We'd have to wait and see.

My grandmother, my mother and I walked into the fire hall prepared to enjoy this tradition at about six. By 6:05, I knew from looking out over the sea of bingo players sitting in their historic seats that it might not be the bowl of jolly laughter my mom had hoped for to distract my visiting grandmother.

We walked up and down the aisles of long tables, empty-handed when others had whole luggage carts of things with them. We finally settled on a table halfway to the back of the room to play the traditional Christmas Eve bingo game, me between my mom and grandmother like the buffer I'd been signed up for.

And then I was promptly assaulted by an angry woman with a bingo bag.

"Tallie Graver, you move your tushy right now. This here is my seat!"

I jumped up before anything else could be said and found another seat another row back. Then I was moved again. By the third move, I was ready to take on any of these grandmas and chain myself to one of the folding chairs, even if my headstone would read "Tallie Graver,

Death by Dauber." I was sure my dad would direct a beautiful funeral and have Mortimer Smith down the road carve me a lovely headstone.

I wasn't complaining too much, though. I'd already been moved three times away from my mother and my grandmother, so I was out of harm's way. I hadn't counted on those women who had been playing for fifty-seven years, every Tuesday without fail, and always sat in the same seat, but I should have.

My grandmother was old enough and had lived here her whole life, before moving to Florida five years ago, to simply turn around and give the demanding you-stole-my-seat accuser the mom-eye. Each one backed away, apologizing. Grumbling the whole way, but still apologizing first.

With her steel-gray hair pulled into a severe bun, the woman was not to be trifled with. It was probably one of the reasons my mom could be such a softy. I would be too if I'd grown up with someone who could stop someone in their tracks with one disdainful glance.

I, however, was not in that age group, nor had I achieved the level of evil eye that Jane Moreland had at eighty-five. For many reasons, I had never gone up against my mother's mother for anything, even when I was too little to understand what that meant. There was just something about the forbidding woman that made you walk on tiptoes. So I had made my way through life preferring to stay under her radar. Even my ex-husband, Walden Phillips III, had never tried to take her on, and that was saying something.

But I was supposed to be the buffer between the two

women this evening. She was my grandmother, and I had agreed to support my mom, Karen Graver, while Jane was here for the next ten days. Ten long days.

Getting moved meant I still got points for being in the firehouse playing bingo, but I didn't have to be next to Grams while she kvetched about every person in the room and even some who were long dead.

I ended up between Alice Mudge, the sweetest woman in town, and Ronda Hogart, probably one of the meanest. Sweet Alice was also a little crazy, but I'd take that any day over the constant sneer on Ronda's face.

This was going to be so. Much. Fun. I almost wished I had put my foot down and told my mother I wasn't going tonight because my boyfriend, Max Bennett, was here for our first Christmas Eve, and I wanted to spend it with him and just him. Instead, he'd come with us and was currently wandering around, looking at all the food on the laden tables against the walls. My best friend, Gina Laudermilch, had outdone herself, along with the pizza shop down the street and the diner at the edge of town.

"It's so nice to see you, Tallie," Alice said, straightening her hunter-green cardigan with its snowman pin and smiling with her whole face.

"Just stay out of my way, girl." Ronda was also my great-aunt or something like that on my mom's side. It was a foggy situation, as with many people in town. Really, any relative older than you became an aunt or uncle, and anyone your age was usually called a cousin.

I only knew that the same blood ran through our veins, and that made us family to some extent. And it was expected that you would tolerate, if not exactly cherish those blood relatives. So I had to be nice to her even if she wasn't someone I specifically looked for to spend any time with.

"Happy Holidays to both of you," I answered. "Hopefully, there are some good prizes tonight."

Alice's smile widened and Aunt Ronda just snorted, then said, "Why did Christmas have to fall on a Wednesday this year? All you interlopers playing at my game and cutting my chances of winning. It's a disgrace. They should have closed it to all you toe-dippers and left it to the people who are committed. There'd better be some cash prizes or I'm taking it up with Howard."

Howard Allerman was the mayor of our little burg. And I had no doubt she'd do just that. Christmas Eve tended to be more of a basket bingo event where, instead of money, you walked away with a basket full of goodies. I would have preferred cash too, but I probably wouldn't win tonight, so it didn't matter. Part of me hoped to win just to make Ronda mad, but the other part wanted to get out of here without the wicked queen of bingo breathing venom down my neck.

Looking around the huge fire hall festooned in swags of evergreen branches and red ribbon, I finally zeroed in on my boyfriend. When we'd walked in, I'd sent Max on a mission: to buy me something to get me through sitting between my mother and my grandmother. Now I might need him to head down to the bar on the corner if I had to sit between these two. I wouldn't even be here if my mom hadn't begged.

Mom turned around at that point with her brow crinkled. I could hear Grams talking from here, even though I couldn't make out what she was saying. It must have been something mean, because my mom looked like she was going to scream. I shrugged at her and pointed to my two seatmates. The little hooligan smiled like the Grinch standing at the top of the mountain making plans to ruin the Whos' Christmas.

Well, at least I didn't feel so bad now.

So here I was, sitting on a metal chair at a plastic table, waiting for the girl to come around with the cards. Alice, to my right, would probably play six to ten cards at the same time, and Aunt Ronda would ultimately have to top her with at least twelve, because it was two games on a card and that was a whole lot of games.

And me? Well, I'd be lucky to keep track of one card with two games.

On either side of me, the two ladies started pulling out all manner of things from their custom tote bags. Bags that were emblazoned with the words BINGOQUEEN in very precise and brightly colored embroidery. Bags that had holsters stuffed with all their good-luck tokens. Bags that were their lives.

Why did I have to get stuck next to the Bingo Queens? And how many queens could there be in our little town? It was a nightmare come true. And then a third one walked over with her own bag absolutely bulging with all manner of things.

"Why, hello, Ronda," Jenna Front said, lowering her bag to the table next to the older woman.

"Seat's taken, go away." Ronda didn't even look up at her.

Jenna's face went stony. "There's no one here."

"There might be, and I'd prefer it to be anyone but you." Aunt Ronda placed her bag on the chair. "I have four kids, not five, and certainly not six. Whatever that rat of a husband of mine has said or done before, that's not going to change just because of what he wants. Now, don't bother me. We've had our words. Go bother some-one else."

Jenna left in a huff and I almost got up to follow her. She'd recently signed on for my cleaning crew, so I felt responsible for her.

I put my hands on the table and started to rise when Ronda's heavy hand fell hard on my shoulder. "Don't you dare. Tina should be around soon with the cards and I won't have you making the game later than it already is. She'll be fine. She's just in a tiff."

"But she's a friend, and that way you and Alice can sit next to each other like you normally do." I tried to make it sound convincing, but she wasn't buying it.

"You need to make better choices in friends. Now sit and stay."

I almost barked at her to tell her I understood and wanted my treat for obeying her orders. My mother chose that moment to turn around again and shake her head at me. Fine, but I was going to leave as soon as I could then.

Troll dolls were set precisely in between little angel statues and small stones. Everything was geared toward good luck and the ultimate prize of being able to yell "bingo" and walk away with lots of money, or baskets in tonight's case.

They both took out round containers with little colored

discs rimmed with metal to use to mark their cards. They also had magnetic wands to collect them when the game was over. I had nothing like that and sheepishly pulled the red-and-white cardboard French fry boat of dried corn toward me.

Tina Metzger finally came around with the cards, thank heavens. Alice pulled her six with wild abandon, almost flinging them all over the carefully set-up table. I took the top one from the stack when she was done.

"Thanks, Tina. How's your son?" I asked.

"We don't have time for chitchat, Tallulah. Take your card and let her move along. She's late as it is."

No one but my father called me Tallulah, and that was only when he was irritated with me. I shouldn't have been surprised that Ronda used my full name now.

"We'll talk later, Tallie." Tina gave me a pained smile as Ronda took the whole stack out of her hands and very carefully laid out four stacks of ten, then cut the decks in half and removed the middle three from each.

Oh, yeah, it was going to be a long night.

But then Max dropped off a funnel cake absolutely covered in powdered sugar and a kiss on my cheek just as the bingo caller at the front of the room turned on the microphone with a high-pitched whine.

Bill Jacobson, the minister at the First Presbyterian two streets up, laughed, and it boomed throughout the high-ceilinged building. "I'd say let's get ready to rumble, but I think that's a different sport."

Right, one that wouldn't involve as much blood and foul language as I expected to fly around tonight.

And then we were off. We didn't have one of those

fancy automatic ball machines; we still had the metal roll cage that had to be hand-cranked. Jenna's husband, Nathan Front, from down at the hardware store, sat with his sleeves rolled up next to Pastor Jacobson. He cranked and he cranked, and then the pastor pulled out the first ball: "O-63."

The numbers were called out fast and furious. I had a hard time keeping up, but Alice and Ronda were throwing down the disks on their cards like they were master blackjack dealers in Vegas.

"B-7." Pastor Jacobson held up the ball, then placed it in the slot in front of him about ten minutes later.

The woman in front of us stood up and screamed, "Bingo!" like her hair was on fire. A chorus of groans went up and the foul language started next to me as Aunt Ronda whisked her wand over her twelve cards, then squeezed off the little chips into her container, muttering words my mom would have washed my mouth out over even at almost thirty if she heard me use them.

I looked around for where Jenna had landed, but didn't see her. I'd catch up with her later and share this incredibly funny experience with her, maybe over tea with Gina. I had to make sitting here worth it somehow.

"Oh, Ronda, watch your language. There are more games in store and you wouldn't have wanted that basket anyway. Look at it, it's filled with those baking pans and oven mitts. You don't even cook!" Alice reached across me to smack Ronda's hand, and I worried that it might be the last thing she'd ever do.

Instead, Ronda shook her head like an angry dog and got herself set back up. I had almost expected spittle to fly from the corners of her mouth. Ah, well, it was still early in the game.

I took a bite of my funnel cake and smiled around it as if enjoying it, but instead I was enjoying the moment. Maybe a little too much, as I missed the first call of the next game.

Things were hopping after that. Games were won and lost. Alice got the basket from the bakery, which made her squeal, and I found that if I paid attention for the most part, I could people watch while I played my one card. The room was full tonight with all manner of citizens from our town and a few people I didn't know. Ronda's husband, Hoagie, who owned the hardware store, buzzed by with a smile to hand her a drink. She snorted at him and shooed him away.

I watched with a smile as my mom's cousin Velma flirted with a guy at the snack stand. Two men in suits I didn't recognize walked the perimeter of the fire hall, then greeted the woman who ran the shoe repair shop on Locust with a hug. Uncle Sherman, the fire chief, waved to me and Chief of Police Burton sent a terse nod my way.

Fortunately, it had been months since I'd had to have very much interaction with Burton. No one had gone toes up when they weren't supposed to recently, so I could mostly stay out of his hair. Of course, we still had people who were passing away. My dad was as busy as ever at the funeral home that had been in our family for generations, but for the most part they'd lived full, long lives, not died under mysterious circumstances. And I hadn't found them. That was a win-win situation as far as I was concerned.

Maybe it wasn't such a bad night after all.

Ronda wasn't having the best of nights, though, and her husband, Uncle Hoagie, had to force her hand down at the last moment when she picked up one of her troll dolls and cocked back her arm to throw it at the pastor. Hoagie only managed to delay the action, because she chucked it hard as soon as he walked away. The pastor knew enough to duck when it came zooming right at his head.

Alice chuckled from her seat next to me. "I told them they should put up the chicken-wire cage tonight, even if it is Christmas Eve, but they didn't listen to me. Pastor Jacobson is getting more agile, though. Last week it hit him in the eye and he had to give his sermon Wednesday night with a big old shiner." She chuckled again. "You missed the B-3, dear."

She put one of her disks on my card, and lo and behold, I had bingo! I shot out of my seat like there was a firecracker under me.

Alice clapped and Ronda gave Grams a run for her money with the death glare she sent my way. Especially because it was the last game and she hadn't won a single game all night long.

"Lousy interlopers. Shouldn't even be allowed to play. Lucky greenhorn." Each derogatory phrase and some others that contained those words my mother would kill me for saying was punctuated by her sweeping her arm across the table and scooping everything into her tote bag.

Uncle Hoagie ran over to help her when she was done and she shoved him out of the way. His face fell. Sliding a hand over his brow, he slicked back his sparse hair and raised his bushy eyebrows. The mole above his eye got a vigorous rub and then he walked in the opposite direction. Poor guy.

"Stomping" was a light word for the way Ronda pushed and shoved her way out of the hall and through the back door. It all happened so fast, I hadn't even gotten around to moving from my place at the table yet.

I glanced toward Alice and she shrugged her shoulders. Moving my gaze to where Ronda had sat, I saw that in her fury and haste, she'd left her purse on the chair next to her.

"Did you see Hoagie?" I asked Alice, really not wanting to do the right thing here and go after Ronda with her purse. Giving it to Uncle Hoagie to give to his irate wife would be far better than chasing after her.

"Nope. You'd better go get your prize, though, before someone else tries to steal it. And I'd watch my back on your way to your house if I were you. I know it's a short walk, but it could be a treacherous one, if you know what I mean." She chuckled and kept packing up her own things. It wasn't the same laugh as before, that jovial, fun one. This one had a slight tinge to it that made the hair on the back of my neck stand up.

"Okay, then. Well, I'd better get this out to . . ." But Alice was already gone with her bag of luck that hadn't gotten her much tonight.

Max approached, looking like someone I could get to do this errand for me.

"Hey, Tallie, great win tonight. Now you can take me out to dinner." He smiled at me and I smiled back.

"Can you go give this to Ronda?" I held up her purse. "She went out the back."

His face pulled into an adorable frown that had me frowning too. "I promised I'd help break down the tables. Maybe you can catch her. I heard the parking lot is a mad-house."

Well, darn it. I was going to have to face the evil queen of bingo anyway.

Better to make it quick and be done. Maybe I would find Uncle Hoagie first. That would work.

With that in mind, I headed out the back door, the way I'd seen Ronda go. Everyone else was heading out the bay doors out front, so of course she'd had to be the odd one.

I couldn't remember what kind of car she drove, but I'd probably find her by her yelling at people to get out of her way so she could get home and practice her throw for next time.

Preparing to step out into the brisk winter air, I wished I had grabbed my coat and possibly my prize. I could have left Ronda's purse with the pastor or even with Uncle Sherman, but my roots were showing and I just couldn't leave it with someone else.

The door latch turned in my hand easily enough, but the door stuck on something. I shoved it hard to get it to open, leaning into it with my considerable weight. It finally moved, only to have a very dead Ronda flop around the edge with a dent in her head and a very blank expression on her lifeless face.

"Tallie, you left without your winnings," my grand-mother said from behind me as I stood there with my mouth hanging open and registering very little. "I got them for you. That's very bad form when the men and women who were generous enough to put this on would like to go home to their families on Christmas Eve. We need to talk about your manners, young lady." She paused to take a breath. It caught in her throat. "Oh my heavens, is that Ronda?"

"Bingo."

Chapter Two

Grams screamed at a frequency I was sure would set off the dogs living next door. They must have been inside for the night, because I didn't hear a single howl to accompany my grandmother's continued caterwauling. The woman had a set of lungs on her, because she hadn't stopped to take a breath yet. I was almost curious to see how long she could go.

But first I had to deal with finding yet another dead body. It was becoming like a habit, and one that Police Chief Burton was not going to be happy about. Again.

I checked for a pulse just as my grandmother finally ran out of breath. Turning to her, I checked to make sure she hadn't just fainted.

"Can you please go see if Burton is still here?" I asked as calmly as I possibly could with my hand on the dead woman's throat.

"But . . . but . . . Ronda." She pointed at the dead woman on the ground as if I hadn't already seen her.

No pulse meant that she was completely dead, not just almost dead or nearly dead but actually dead, and on Christmas Eve.

I didn't touch anything else. Grams turned back into the fire hall and Max stepped out around her.

"Oh, babe," he said as he crouched down beside me.

"Yeah. Grams is getting Burton. Don't touch anything. I don't want to get in trouble for messing up the scene, because this is most definitely a murder. Look at the dent in her head. You don't get that from opening the door wrong."

"No, I don't suppose you do." Burton, dressed in jeans and a plaid vest with a Christmas tree handkerchief in the pocket walked around Max and crouched down next to me too. We formed a circle around the poor dead woman.

"I don't know when this happened or how." I stood up, because my knees were starting to hurt. "All I wanted to do was give her the purse she forgot, but then I found her like this."

Burton put a hand on my shoulder. "Always something, isn't it, Tallie?"

Recently, Burton and I had started having coffee every once in a while when we happened to be at Gina's coffee shop at the same time. Slowly but surely, we'd built on the small start we'd made months ago when I'd almost died at the hands of a crazy woman bent on turning our little town into some kind of criminal circus. Everything wasn't always awesome of course, and he still found me irritating sometimes, or gave me tickets just because he could. But for the most part we'd come to an understanding. He seemed to believe, finally, that I wasn't trying to take his job when I figured out who was murdering people and why in our little town.

But I'd do anything to stay out of his way. No matter that I'd started listening to some podcasts he'd recommended about past crimes around the world and we'd had some lively discussions over lattes and sticky buns.

This was the first murder since we'd gotten on better footing and I wasn't sure how he was going to react to me finding yet another body. I prepared myself for anything.

"I'm thinking someone hit her in the head with the varnish can to your left." He pulled a pen from his pocket and lifted up the handle on a can marked with a Mr. Yuk sticker and Hogart's Hardware on the side. "We have to find Hoagie."

"We?" I said before I could stop myself.

"Maybe this time you'll just use the tip line like normal concerned citizens, but I have a feeling that's not actually going to happen. So if you find out something, let me know, but don't go actively looking for a criminal again. It gives me heart palpitations no matter how much I ultimately have to appreciate the information at the end."

Well, that was quite an endorsement. "I, uh, don't know what to say."

"That's a first. Let's see if it lasts." His grunt wasn't as irritated as it usually was as he looked over Ronda Hogart's dead body. "Call Suzy if you can and tell her to get the guys down here. I guess we're working on Christmas Eve after all."

There wasn't much for me to do once the rest of our small police force came and the EMTs showed up from down the street. Max and I headed back to our apartment above my parents' funeral home on the other side of the firehouse. Christmas lights sparkled across the street in Gina's coffee shop display window. She'd made an elaborate show of trains and lights and tiny Christmas trees. A whole village sat at the base of a mountain made of fake whipped cream, and delicate china cups filled with fake hot chocolate skied down the slope. She'd taken the ski slopes five miles up the road and had lovingly recreated them along the width of her store.

Smart lady. I loved her creativity and her passion for what she did. And I hoped she'd soon be my sister-in-law, if my brother ever got his head together and did the right thing.

After months of telling her that they should get married and hiding behind the excuse that it would look better for his reputation, he'd suddenly stopped asking and had become secretive about a month ago. I didn't know what he had up his sleeve, but I hoped it was a ring and a spectacular display, the kind my best friend deserved.

For now, though, I had my newly renovated top penthouse suite above the dead to enjoy.

Those television shows about home renovations were entirely misleading. Sure, sometimes they broke out a wall and found a hornet's nest, or gobs of mold. But we only got to see their remodeling done in segments, in a montage that only showed the progress, not the swearing and the tempers.

But as with everything I did, our renovation of the third floor of my parents' funeral home had been far more complicated, to say the least. For instance, take the horror of finding the floor in the section that had previously been my bedroom had been held up for however many years with broken paint sticks and bubble wrap under a spot I'd always avoided because it felt soft. Or the half a stop sign shoved under a floorboard to make it float where a vent used to be. And let's not forget the chimney someone had collapsed years ago when they'd put on a new roof. Instead of removing it when they had the chance, they'd made all the bricks fall into the chimney itself for the top five feet, leaving birds' nests in there and some sort of tiny skeleton I didn't want to put a name to.

Max and I had shoveled out any number of things, stripped what felt like miles of floor, scraped off wallpaper until our arms hurt and moved mountains of antique furniture. And before it was done we would probably end up hiring a contractor to finish things up, as I had wanted from the beginning. In the meantime, Max was flexing his renovator muscles.

The object had been to make it into a real, livable space instead of the cramped one room I'd been making do with for almost the last two years. And it wasn't turning out half bad. Or at least I didn't think it would be bad once it was finally done.

Dealing with my family up close and personal after all those years of separating myself from them during my marriage had not been easy, but Max made it better and far more tolerable. And now that he actually lived here instead of hours away in Washington, DC, I was incredibly happy.

Despite ripping up carpet and moving trunks of clothes from over a hundred years ago, we'd had fun and hadn't killed each other. Yet.

Because the work wasn't yet finished, I didn't even have a tree up or a single Christmas light. We weren't without cheer and my electric bill would at least be lower.

Those were the pluses. The minuses were that even with it being the day before Christmas, I didn't quite feel like it should even be December at this point.

Max and I had been busy ever since he'd moved in. Between renovations and trying to get his tax business up and running, we had been on the go nonstop. He'd rented a back office from Hoagie on the second floor of the hardware store, but the clients weren't exactly pouring in, much to my disappointment, and with the renovations, he'd decided to take a break over the holidays to get our penthouse done. Although it probably had given us too much time to yell at each other over paint colors and whether or not to varnish the floors or install carpet.

I won with the carpet and looked forward to how plush it would be under my feet as I stepped out of my flats and into the living room.

Max smiled as he opened the door to our third-floor al-most paradise and I stood in the doorway, not sure if I could believe what before my wandering eyes should appear but a fully decorated living room.

"What? When? How?" Calling myself baffled would have been an understatement. I was completely over-whelmed by the beauty that was currently on display in my new living room. Small ceramic Christmas trees all aglow that I hadn't seen in years, twinkling lights gar-landing every window, a huge tree with my dog Peanut and my cat Mr. Fleefers nestled in their respective beds and bows around their necks. Well, they weren't in their actual respective beds because Mr. Fleefers was sprawled in the Saint Bernard's bed and poor Peanut had cramped herself and overflowed from the small rectangle that should have held the small, black-and-gray cat.

I turned to Max with a smile that almost hurt because it was so wide.

"All the decorations your mother was willing to spare, tonight before we went to bingo while you were getting one of your absolutely necessary whoopie pie concoctions and with a lot of help from your brothers Jeremy and Dylan." He looked monumentally pleased with himself and I couldn't blame him.

Running to hug him seemed the only right thing to do. So I did.

We stayed that way for just a moment before I heard a siren from the firehouse next door.

"So I guess Uncle Sherman will be working tonight, along with Burton, two different cases on what's supposed to be one of the best nights of the year." I rested my head on Max's broad chest. "Do you think they at least found Hoagie?"

"I don't know." He kissed the top of my head. "Let's put it away for tonight at least. Can we? I have a present for you, and I'm sure when Burton has something he needs you to know, he'll let you know."

I snorted, but let it go after that. I had a present for Max too and sincerely hoped he liked it.

After Max lit the candles around the faux fireplace we'd picked up for a song at a discount store, we sat on our recently purchased couch.

I hid his present behind my back, but he had mine on his lap. It was a big box and I felt like my little wrapped package was probably not going to stack up against whatever he had in store for me.

"I'm going first," I said, because if my gift for him

was a disappointment, at least I'd get to enjoy my own for just a moment before he frowned. He handed it over and I was like a toddler, ripping paper with abandon to find that he had bought me one of those roaming vacuum cleaners.

I burst out laughing. "You know how much I don't trust these things."

"And I also know that our living space has almost quadrupled and I thought it might be nice not to have to worry about dog hair all the time."

"Okay, points for that, I guess." I took it out and tried to think of it in good terms instead of worrying that I'd trip over it all the time and feel like it was watching me.

And now it was my turn. I was no longer afraid to hand him his gift, so I presented it with a flourish. His face lit up like a giddy child's and I started worrying again.

He grabbed the package and opened it carefully, sliding his finger under each piece of tape, gently lifting each corner of the paper until I wanted to rip it out of his hands and demolish the thing. I bit my tongue instead.

And then it was done. "A Pennsylvania Dutch cookbook?"

Or maybe that was just what sounded like a question mark at the end of his sentence. He had a big old smile on his face and hugged me. "I'm thinking this is a request for more home-cooked meals in our big, newly outfitted kitchen?"

"Well . . ."

He laughed and laughed. "I guess I should have known when you gave me carte blanche in the restaurant store."

I thought about the other things I'd watched him ogle

in that store and the mental list I'd made and then used to buy a lot of his gifts. What else was a girl to do for a guy who seemed to have one of everything? Or at least that was what I'd thought when he and all his worldly possessions had pulled up in the moving truck three months ago.

We'd started renovating the house days later and were frequent visitors to Hoagie's hardware store down the street.

And just like that, my mood dampened. "Poor Hoagie and his family. To lose your mother on the night before Christmas, no matter how mean she could be. It's like that song with the grandmother getting run over by a reindeer, but worse. My cousins must be devastated."

Max hugged me. "Well, at least you waited until after the presents before diving right back in." And then he laughed. "Bring on the discussion."

I sat cross-legged on the couch and pulled a pillow onto my lap. "Someone smacked Aunt Ronda in the head with a can of varnish hard enough to kill her. A can of varnish from their hardware store." Conveniently, there was a plate of my mom's snickerdoodles set out on the end table with a note for Santa. I reached for them and grabbed a few. I'd replace them later after my thinking time.

Max angled himself to play with my hair and face me. "Right. So you think it was a moment of anger? Something she said? Or did? I can't imagine it was premeditated. Although where did the varnish can come from?"

I sat for a moment, not wanting to say what I was actually thinking.

"Do you think Hoagie was the one who killed her?"

Max must either have read my mind, or my thoughts were more obvious than I wanted them to be.

I shook my head after a moment. "I just can't imagine that. Uncle Hoagie has been a fixture in my life since I was born. I've watched him put up with all kinds of things from Ronda, and as far as I know, he has never hurt her. Why tonight?" I went on before Max could answer. "No, I think maybe someone was just waiting to get her alone for all of her meannesses. Or maybe to pay her back for all her bingo bitchery?"

"That seems a little violent for a game of cardboard cards and dried corn."

I scoffed. "Oh that's nothing, the chicken-wire cage was missing tonight at bingo simply because it's Christmas. Pastor Jacobson has had cards thrown at him, trolls, glass angels, daubers and even a beer bottle or two on BYOB nights when they didn't like the numbers he called."

"You can't be serious." His fingers stilled in my hair and I smiled at his naiveté.

"Very serious. It's why I avoid bingo as often as possible."

"No doubt."

"But why on Christmas Eve?" The clock struck midnight. "I think I'm going to have to sleep on it."

"Ready to have sweet dreams of Christmas?"

"Either that or insightful dreams about murder." Really, I was up for either one. Had Burton found Hoagie? How had he taken it? The guy would probably be devastated no matter what.

Did we have their funeral arrangements? I couldn't imagine that someone who was related to us, no matter how distantly, would choose to go somewhere else, but it had happened before; rarely, but it had. I'd have to check tomorrow if I could get a moment to run downstairs without tipping off Max that I was going to look into this on Christmas Day of all days.

There were worse things I could be doing.

Chapter Three

Nothing insightful came to me during the night, and I did everything I could to keep myself from calling Burton first thing in the morning to see if they'd found Hoagie. I so did not want it to be him.

Not to mention it was Christmas morning, and even Burton should be able to have some time to spend wondering if Santa had given him coal or had taken pity on him for having to deal with me and gotten him a huge new grill, which he'd been talking about over our coffee times.

To distract myself, Max and I opened presents, though nothing as magnificent as my roaming vacuum cleaner, which was currently stuck in the linen closet, bumping against the door. Max did laugh over the skull-and-cross-bones pajamas I got him, and then we nearly fell over laughing when I opened the exact same pajamas from him.

After we ate brunch—one that Max very quickly took the hint to make due to the marked page in his new cookbook and the fact that all the ingredients were conveniently available in the new silver refrigerator—Max took a nap while I talked myself into doing one of the Sudoku puzzles he'd gotten me.

But after about twenty minutes, I just couldn't contain myself. Checking over my shoulder to make sure Max was still napping on the couch, I pulled up the internet and went on the hunt for any information regarding Ronda Hogart's death.

On the local paper's website there was a brief mention that she had passed away and that anyone with information could contact the police. They had a picture of her that must have been taken forty years ago with her then-brown Farrah Fawcett hair, huge glasses rimmed in red, and teal eye shadow. She looked younger certainly, but not a lot happier.

I went back to the search page and there wasn't much more about her. Some mentions of the hardware store she and her husband had opened over forty years ago, a few monumental bingo wins, and a mention of Hoagie running a 5K back in the nineties, but no more pictures. Not a single one. No social media presence for the store, not even a listing on those sites that help you find stores for certain services in your area. That was curious, but not unheard of in our little town.

Maybe I could ask my mom if she had any pictures when we had dinner with the family this afternoon. We were due at my parents' house in a few hours for Christmas dinner, a tradition in the Graver family for as long as I could remember. And one I wasn't going to miss, no matter how much I wanted to continue to look for information on the Hogarts.

We'd have turkey and mashed potatoes, cranberry sauce, broccoli with cheese sauce, corn soufflé and stuffing that made my mouth water just thinking about it. My mom would make a dessert that did not include sprinkles, and eggnog was strictly forbidden as a drink choice, after that unfortunate incident with Aunt Mildred in 1982.

This was only my second Christmas dinner in more years than I wanted to count, so I looked forward to it with much gastric anticipation, even if it meant my mom would hover, my dad would drill me about when I might be ready to come work in the family business full-time and one brother would give me the evil eye for not being more involved in the family business no matter how much he loved me. The other one didn't cause me any trouble, but Jeremy Graver liked to test the limits of my patience with his high-and-mighty act and was good at tipping me over the line.

At least I wouldn't have to microwave something again or try to find a restaurant I hadn't eaten at ten times in the three months since Max's move. With only three days of a working stovetop and oven, I didn't know when I might ever again want to eat somewhere that brought my food to me on plates that weren't mine. I happily did the dishes just to be able to know what exactly was in the food I was eating. Plus, Christmas was horrendous for reservations unless you made them months ahead. And I did not want Chinese food.

So my mother's house was a most welcome distraction

for the evening, and seeing my family would be a blast once we got there.

I gave up trying to find more information or distract myself and took a book and a blanket to the chair and a half Max had insisted on putting in front of the bay window overlooking the street. With the additional square footage, I no longer had to worry about cramming everything together and had some space to spread out. It was good, and the sun felt warm on my neck as I read, petted Peanut and got the ultimate shun from my cat, Mr. Fleefers.

The church bells rang out two streets over and I jumped out of the chair, disrupting Peanut and making Mr. Fleefers hiss. I looked at my watch just to verify the time and realized I'd lost track of time while I was trying not to research more online, instead getting lost in my book.

We were supposed to be there in fifteen minutes. Yikes!

"Let's get a move on!" I yelled across the gigantic living room that used to be my entire living area. Peanut jumped about a foot, which created a different kind of noise, and Mr. Fleefers sauntered over to the front window as if none of this concerned him in the least.

"Holy crap!" Max yelled back, falling off the couch in a tumble of blankets.

"Now, Max. We have fifteen minutes!"

Max emerged from under the pile of blankets like he probably would for the rest of our days. His brown hair stuck straight up off his head and he had blanket creases on the side of his face. His shirt was askew and his sweatpants were bunched up around his knees.

I smiled at the picture he made and he smiled back, his dimple winking at me.

"Get in the shower, you ridiculous man. I'll call my mom to let her know it's going to be a little bit."

He kissed me on his way to the bathroom and gave me a quick squeeze. I appreciated that because I was ready to walk out the door now, already washed and ready to go, styled like a boss in my new ugliest sweater yet. Festooned with ribbons, and an angry cat that looked suspiciously like Mr. Fleefers wrapped in Christmas lights that actually lit up, it was not only garish and over-the-top, it was magnificent and would make my father groan. Bonuses all around. And a far cry from the elegant dresses and heels and diamonds I'd worn when I was married to my ex-husband, Walden Phillips III. I loved every inch of it and every second of my life since I'd walked out on him, no matter how many hard days there'd been.

The call to my mom wasn't as bad as I thought it would be because my uncle Sherman was also going to be late, so she had pushed dinner back another thirty minutes.

True to his word, it only took a few minutes for Max to be all sparkly clean and presentable. In stark contrast to my dazzling display, Max was outfitted in a subtle green, long-sleeved, button-down shirt with a lovely paisley tie and matching vest. His shoes were shiny, his hair perfect, his pants neatly pressed.

"Where has that been?" I asked as I straightened his tie. It didn't really need to be straightened; I just wanted to touch him. Having him here instead of constantly waiting for him to visit from Washington, DC, was such a treat, and the fact that he was here to stay made my heart very happy.

"Your mom opened up the closet on the second floor for some of my business clothes now that I haven't needed them. It feels good to be back in something other than jeans."

"Missing the corporate world?"

"Not at all, but it's Christmas, and I've been stuck at mandatory office parties with stuffy people in appropriate business attire for the last fifteen years. I like dressing up every once in a while. And I appreciate your family."

And I knew how much they appreciated him. Relations between us had improved vastly since Max had come back into our lives. He hadn't ever really left my brother, Jeremy's, but he'd only recently come back on a more permanent basis for the rest of us, and we were all much better for it.

I was getting gushy and needed to stop before I said something that would make us even later and my makeup run off my face.

We hopped in the car and headed over to my parents' house, a few blocks away. We could have walked, but more often than not, I was sent away from there with left-overs galore and I didn't want to have to carry them home even a few blocks. Plus, there would be presents. And there was snow; a lot of snow on the side streets the snowplows hadn't yet come to move off the road.

About half a block down, I yelled for Max to pull over. I'd seen a flyer tacked to the telephone pole, which was a big no-no in the borough. I thought maybe it was about a lost dog or cat. The people who policed those flyers weren't totally cold-hearted and would leave them up for a little while. It was the garage sale signs they hated. But since it wasn't garage-sale time and the picture was definitely not of an animal, I'd looked a little closer as Max had crept by on the unplowed road. And it was Hoagie Hogart on a missing persons poster.

I jumped out of the car in my heeled boots and hustled back the few strides to the sign. A blurry picture of the man who had run the hardware store forever, and one I hadn't seen online, was stuck to the telephone pole with a nail. It was on flimsy paper and had a contact number at the bottom. It simply said he was missing and asked that anyone let them know if they found him. I took out my phone and quickly punched the number into my contacts list. It wasn't one from the police station, and I wondered if it was a cousin's number.

I'd been tempted to rip the thing off the telephone pole and take it with me, but I didn't want to keep anyone else from seeing it if it was the trigger that found the man, who must still be missing.

Burton hadn't told me that, but I also hadn't asked.

"What's up?" Max asked when I got back into the car.

"Hoagie is still missing. They have signs up."

"That was quick."

I shrugged. "It might be because Burton is pressing to find him to answer questions about what happened last night. He walked out before Ronda, presumably to start the car so the queen wouldn't be cold." I shouldn't have spoken ill of the dead, but sometimes it was unavoidable. "Sorry. I wouldn't want to be cold either, and it was chilly last night. Anyway, he must have gone out to start the car, but then she was killed and he was nowhere to be found. I wonder if his car is gone too."

I made a mental note to ask Burton if they still hadn't found Uncle Hoagie tomorrow. It was burning my brain not to be able to find out what was going on, but I promised myself this day with Max and my family. And ultimately, it wasn't actually my job to find murderers. Burton was doing his job; I had to believe that.

"I wonder if the store will be open this week. I was going to go into the office later, but if the whole store is closed, I won't be able to get in. I only have a key to the interior door." Max pulled back onto the road and continued our short journey.

"That is brilliant!" When Max had moved here, Hoagie had offered him some empty office space he had in the store so Max could set up a desk and a visitor's chair so he could be official to start looking for clients. Business wasn't exactly booming yet, but Max said he was fine with that because he wanted to get settled before he started working hard again. And with the holidays, he'd decided to take some time off. So, with the office in the hardware store, that would give us access to all things Hogart. Like I said, brilliant.

From Max's quizzical look, I figured that was not the response he had expected. "Thanks?"

I turned in my seat. "No, if we can't find Hoagie, we can at least go in to see what's going on, maybe explore a little in other offices."

His quizzical look turned into a frown. Oops, time to change the subject. "Well, hopefully they're open for you, so you can get your info together to start advertising for new business."

Not a great save, but then we arrived at my mother's and I was able to instead ooh and ahh over their decorations.

In contrast to the brick and mortar that held together the funeral home on Main Street, Bud and Karen Graver's house was stone and powder-blue siding. They'd upgraded it over the years, adding a sunporch on the back for entertaining, per my mom. Being the funeral director in town, my dad wanted people to know him before he became necessary, and my mother loved to cook. To that end, they had barbecues and picnics and formal dinners at least once a month. And weekly it was our family's time to sit down around the table. Tonight was special, though.

The house was absolutely covered in lights, enough to give Clark Griswold a run for his money. I was sure my dad hadn't done it himself; that was my brother Dylan's job every year. And every year it became more extravagant. In fact, as we entered the driveway, I spotted a new scene that Dylan must have picked up for the holidays this year—an eight-foot-tall North Pole blow-up globe with elves, reindeer, Santa's workshop and candy canes all aglow and moving in time with the flashing lights. I was sure the entire neighborhood loved being blinded by the cavorting creatures. My dad probably had a fit when he came home to find the whole thing nearly blocking his driveway. I hadn't heard about it yet, so I was assuming Dylan had just put it up. Maybe an early Christmas present. It made me smile no matter when it was put up.

Parking the car, we sat for just a moment.

"Thank you for being here," I said as the engine ticked.

"I wouldn't miss it for the world. You really can't understand how much it means to me to be here like this."

"Even with the chaos of my family, the tight community and the fact that you don't have a ton of clients yet for your new Taxinator business?"

He turned to me and put his hand on my cheek. "The clients will come when they're ready. Tax season hasn't even started yet and I'm not in any hurry to crunch numbers again at the moment. The chaos of your family is just what I need and the community isn't tight like a noose, but like the family I missed out on growing up."

As we exited the car, I hoped those thoughts stayed in his head as he continued to have to deal with all of us. This was our first Christmas up here and he didn't quite know what he was getting himself into. But he would know just as soon as we walked through the door.

To be truthful, though, I hadn't realized how much I'd missed these dinners until I'd allowed myself to be drawn back into the tradition.

Turning to look at Max, I hooked my arm through his as we walked up from the garage. He was a big part of things now and I couldn't imagine life without him either, much like Peanut, my relatively new dog. Well, more than Peanut, probably. I giggled and thought I probably shouldn't tell Max that.

"What's so funny?"

I kissed his cheek as we hit the back door.

"Aw, now that's what I like to see. Soon enough, maybe the two of you will do the right thing and get married, then give me babies. I want babies in the house again."

My mother never failed to get her wants and needs out on the table as soon as she saw me. But I had seen Jeremy's car out front, and Dylan's. Which meant both my brothers were here to be grilled. If I could just redirect the conversation to Jeremy and Gina and them getting married, or how Dylan needed to get a girlfriend who stayed around longer than a few weeks, I'd be off the hook.

I kissed my mom on the cheek without answering her and walked into what could only be called the chaos I'd referenced earlier.

My dad had on a frilly apron, Gina was carrying dishes to the formal dining room—where I assumed Grams was holding court and directing traffic like a drillmaster—Dylan trailed along behind her with even more food and Jeremy rolled his eyes at me as he passed with a pitcher of what I thought must be sweet tea, the kind you could stand a spoon up in. My teeth ached just looking at it, but that didn't stop my mouth from watering for a taste.

Lights and garland and Christmas villages covered with snow decorated every available surface. The kitchen hutch held my mother's collection of those dreadful elves on the shelves, literally. All three shelves were crammed with the felt and plush concoctions. She'd been an absolutely fiend about using them when we were little. I still had nightmares about finding the things in my shoes, wrapped around my toothbrush and holding my cereal spoon with a death grip one morning.

I glanced at Max to find him smiling. Sometimes I forgot he'd never had this kind of family, and that as much as we fought and argued, we still loved one another. This was probably a wonder of wishing for him, and the next time he talked about marriage, I should give it some real consideration. Not that I'd tell my mother that or she'd break out her calendar, a slew of wedding books and the gown she'd worn over thirty-five years ago.

I'd rather be nearly drowned in a creek again than endure that at the moment.

Time to get cracking on the redirecting of mother-henning.

"So, Dylan," I said as I passed him on his way back to

the kitchen. "No girl this week? I could have sworn I saw you with Macy Yoder making kissy faces at that new Greek restaurant last week."

My mother crowed and ran into the kitchen after him.

Mission accomplished. Now, to eat some good food and laugh until my sides hurt. I was going to have to put away my curiosity about whether or not Hoagie had been found and who had killed Ronda. I was willing to do that with all this food in front of me and my mother on a tangent toward another child.

Christmas with the Gravers was off to a great start.

Chapter Four

The elaborate table my mom had set nearly groaned with food. Her pretty, snowflake-pattern china set was out in full force, along with the crystal goblets etched with a Christmas scene. The napkins were linen with poinsettias on them, and the entire table was covered with a huge Christmas tree tablecloth. Just one tree, covering the whole thing.

My mom was nothing if not thorough.

The potatoes were passed, the corn soufflé dished out generously, the turkey doused in creamy gravy and all was right in the world. I made sure to take good-sized portions because if I didn't, my mother would give me the eye and then heap more on my plate anyway.

Conversation turned to local events after my mother grilled Dylan about his lack of a suitable girlfriend and slam-dunked him with what a nice girl that Macy Yoder was, and how she came from a good family. Grams nodded in approval and put in her own two cents.

He gave me more than one stink eye, but was all too happy to join in when it was time for Jeremy to go under the bus. My best friend, Gina, was the one giving the stink eye when Jeremy placed his napkin carefully on his plate and stated he would propose when he was good and ready.

My dear uncle Sherman was quick to take up the dramatic pause after that announcement and launched into his latest issue as the fire chief.

"I think we have a firebug in town. I need to find him before he hurts anyone. It's a real gosh darn mystery." He cocked an eyebrow at me as he speared a big piece of turkey and shoved it in his mouth.

My mother gasped and put her hand to her throat. "A firebug? What exactly does that mean? It sounds bad."

"Oh, for heaven's sake, Karen. You can't be that dull-witted." Grams took a swig of her tea and made a face of disapproval. "I need water."

Everyone ignored her as I took up the conversation.

"Someone who is setting fires around town, Mom," I jumped in before my grandmother could cut her daughter again. Pushing around some cranberry sauce on my plate, I avoided eye contact. The jellied fruit was not my favorite, but I had taken it anyway when my grandmother cleared her throat as I went to pass it to Max without having put any on my plate.

"Oh, that's even worse! I thought it was some kind of insect."

I loved her, I really did, but what world did she live in? Maybe that hair dye she always used had started messing with her brain synapses.

Grams snorted, very unladylike, as my dad stiffened in his chair.

"Tallie has it right." Sherman saved the day again by stepping right in. "We've had a bunch of fires recently, some little and some big. So far no one's been hurt, but I'm afraid those days are numbered, and I can't seem to figure out who's doing this. It's driving me insane."

"That's unfortunate," my dad said. He speared more broccoli and looked at my plate, where I'd heaped the stuff like I was growing my own forest of broccoli trees. I stabbed one and shoved it in my mouth.

Sitting back, Sherman patted his big stomach. "It's been about three weeks and there's been six fires. They started out smaller and were normal little house calls to make sure everything was okay, but they've escalated lately. I'm afraid Bertie Myers is not going to be able to stay on top of the workload if this keeps up. Not to mention that the officials in town are looking to me to contain this thing."

"Bertie does the fire cleanup?" I asked, vaguely remembering a mention of him when my mother said I might want to look into that if I was bent on cleaning instead of working at the funeral home, as my father had hoped for.

"Yeah, he takes away all the things that aren't destroyed and tries to clean them up so people can keep what few possessions are left. It's a dirty job, but he's a good guy and good at doing it."

"And you don't have any leads on how the fires are starting?" I put my elbows on the table and my chin in my hands to give him my full attention. My mother cleared her throat, and I sat back with my posture straight. Between her and my grandmother, I was pretty sure I wouldn't do a single thing right tonight. Such was life.

"A few, because we think it's got a particular accelerant, but other than that, we're out of information." He shrugged. "Whoever it is has to be clever because no one has seen anything suspicious. Still waiting for some lab results on what they're starting it with, but it looks like each fire has three points of ignition. It's distinct and I want it to stop."

"No doubt, Sherman." My dad put down his fork. "This is troubling, and I've heard around town that they want it solved and fast. It will happen. You've always been able to discern when things aren't right."

"Yeah, well, my discerner is apparently turned off at the moment." He frowned, and I frowned with him. If I could count on one thing in life, it was Uncle Sherman and his jovial disposition. Not being able to protect the town was probably eating at him.

"I'm sorry," I said. "I hope you can get some answers." I reached for the pie in the middle of the table, and my mom was the one frowning this time. Her signal that it wasn't yet time. I sighed.

"Yeah, me too." His eyed narrowed at me, and he leaned his elbows on the table. Not a single noise from my mother or grandmother, which was not fair at all. "And Burton's actually the one who's responsible for all this investigating thing, but it's my territory, and I'm not going to let him screw this up."

"Still have that age-old feud going on? Wasn't that forever ago?" Grams asked.

I flinched, knowing that it had been over a woman who had married Sherman but had left years ago to live on an island, away from both men.

"You need to let that go, old man," my father chimed in before I could say anything more.

"I'm no older than you, Buddy boy."

I closed my eyes for just a second. My father hated being called that, but he laughed this time, which was fortunate. His snowman tie jingled with the noise, probably something my mom had made him wear because he was all about the solid colors on a normal day.

"I'll have you know you're ten months older than me. We'll leave it at that."

"You got me there." Sherman sighed. "I feel old these days. What with all the fires and then how Aunt Mary died, I feel like life is moving right along and leaving me behind."

Aunt Mary had been ninety-two and led an amazing life, still dancing for the local dance studio and competing right up until her last days. Which reminded me that I would need to make sure I put time into my schedule to be there for her funeral. I wasn't a big fan of working at the funeral home owned by my parents, but when it came to family, you put aside whatever resistance you had and made it a priority to be there for those you loved.

And even those you only tolerated.

"If you don't mind making time day after tomorrow,

Tallie, it would be much appreciated." Mom put her hand on top of mine, and I gave her a squeeze.

"Of course."

"Thank you. You're a good girl. You'd be better if you got married, though. I'm just saying."

"She's not wrong. I don't approve of this living together without matrimony, Tallie," Grams said.

Sherman jumped in again before the disastrous duo could get rolling.

"I'm sure Burton's not really going to want your help with Ronda's murder, Tallie, no matter what I heard him say last night. Did he tell you that they still haven't found Hoagie?"

He looked at me skeptically, and I bit my lip.

"Ah, well, he's stupid not to acknowledge all the things you've done for him over the last year or so. These fires might not be a dead person, but they're still very important. Look at all the times you've helped him and I guarantee that cold case file of his would be a whole lot bigger without your help."

Why did I feel like I was being buttered up like one of my mom's amazing, yeasty rolls?

"Thanks. I don't normally want to solve them for him, and I'm not saying he's incompetent. I just don't get why you wouldn't take any help you can get when you're trying to figure out what happened." I speared a slice of cranberry sauce and cut it in half, then in half again. Maybe if I made it really small, my mom wouldn't notice that I hadn't eaten it.

"Completely understood." Sherman smiled at me, and the butter feeling intensified. "He couldn't have solved any of those without you and your keen eye for detail, your knack for picking up things that people leave around and your ear for gossip and eavesdropping."

Buttered.

"I've often been impressed with your attention to detail and your tenaciousness."

Now he was bringing out the big words and laying on the flattery like cream cheese on a freshly toasted bagel.

Even my dad heard it. "What are you getting at, Sherman? Tallie is all those things, but what's your angle here?"

Sherman spread his hands wide, as if he had nothing to hide and nowhere to hide it. "I was just letting her know how much more I think she does than Burton will ever admit."

"I appreciate that, Uncle Sherman, and thanks for the compliments, but even I can see you're aiming at something." I touched my nose with the side of my finger. "That amateur sleuth sniffer, you know."

"Well." Then he paused and looked around the table at everyone who was staring intently at him. "I was just thinking that if you wanted to put some of that sleuthing into action to sniff out any information around town about these arsons, I certainly wouldn't turn you away like Burton does. Every. Single. Time." He accentuated those pauses between the last three words by stabbing his finger into the Christmas tree tablecloth. The last stab was so forceful it made his snowflake plate jump on the table and his glass of sweet tea rattle.

I contemplated the idea as my grandmother squinted her eyes at me. I was a good sleuth, even if I didn't always mean to be a good one. I'd even flirted with the idea of possibly going professional at one time, back when I was still trying to figure out what I wanted to be when I grew up. I knew now because of how much I truly enjoyed my new cleaning crew and the great things we were doing.

So what did Sherman expect me to do? I wouldn't even know where to start with this one.

I opened my mouth to say so when my father cut me off.

"Do you really think you don't have enough to do, young lady?" Dad speared me with a glare. Oh no, we were going to get into the whole why-won't-I-work-for-them-if-I-was-bored thing.

I tried to head him off, but he had a full steam going on and there was no stopping him.

"We need help at the funeral home. You saw what happened a few months ago with overscheduling and understaffing. Your mother and I are worn out and we are seriously considering hiring more outside full-time staff because you won't step up and take your rightful place in the family business."

Jeremy shoved back in his chair and folded his arms tight across his chest. Oh, we were about to get fighty up in here. And Grams just sat there without saying a word. Maybe she didn't know all the things that had gone on. Or maybe I should make her some popcorn so she could enjoy the show she usually missed by living in Florida.

"I told you, I don't think that's necessary. I am willing to take on more, Dad. Dylan and Tallie are free to make their own choices," Jeremy said.

Good for him. I started to smile at him, and then he continued.

"No matter how it affects other people, if they want to selfishly decide to turn their backs on those closest to them who need them, who are we to try to force them to do the right thing?"

I burst from my chair, and so did Dylan. It erupted into a full-out yelling match. I wondered how Max felt about close family now . . .

Chapter Five

"I can help." Max calmly wiped the side of his mouth with his napkin and then folded it nicely before placing it next to his plate. The forest-green of the linen sat in stark contrast to the white snowflake china my mom liked to use for any dinners having to do with winter.

I sat stunned into silence, just like everyone else at the table. He'd effectively cut off the shouting match between us siblings and our father with those three simple words.

I sputtered and then coughed before finding my voice. "But you have an accounting degree and you're my Taxinator. You worked for the government finding nasty people who tried to cheat on what they owed. You did big things. You were going to work on gathering a client list while enjoying our house."

He placed his hand over mine. "And I also have time to help out your family. Now that the renovation is almost done, I will have more time. Besides, depending on the salary I can talk your father into, perhaps we can pay to have an actual contractor come in. I'm less of a handyman than I thought, and handling people and making plans is what I've done for years. This focus is a little different, but still in the service business. I'd be happy to help your parents and my best friend so that you and your other brother can continue to pursue your dreams without inconveniencing anyone."

I followed the direction of his gaze and found him looking directly at Jeremy. While my brother had every right to wish that Dylan and I would fall right into line with his plans, he couldn't expect it, and Max was subtly letting him know that he was out of line without calling him out.

"Max, are you sure?" My dad, Bud Graver, looked simultaneously thankful and yet skeptical. "It's not an easy business. Sometimes the sadness can overwhelm you when dealing with grief-stricken people."

"I'm sure Tallie would be willing to give me some pointers, and I'm willing to learn. When I told her I was looking for a change, I didn't necessarily just mean in scenery. Perhaps this is something I'll excel at. I'm willing to give it a try, especially if it would help you, Bud and Jeremy, and give Dylan and Tallie a pass when it comes to failing to step up in your eyes."

A subtle burn again, but both my father and my brother flinched, so it had struck its mark. I loved cleaning more than I had originally thought I would. When I left Waldo and had no money, it had been the only thing I could come up with to do to make money. And then I realized I liked it. I didn't want to give it up now, especially because I had a whole crew depending on me. I enjoyed serving that way.

And I knew Dylan and my father had been looking at the cemetery up the street, which had just come up for sale, so that he could continue to play outdoors as he loved to.

But did I want to be married to a funeral director? Wasn't it enough that I had been sired by one and was the sister to another? I really wished Max had talked with me before he made his offer.

There was still time for us to talk it out more before it was finalized, I hoped. Scratch that: I'd make sure of it. But no matter what, I would support him just as much as he supported me. It was the way things worked, no matter how much I shied away from the idea of it. I'd figure out how to be happy if he really wanted to do this, as opposed to doing it to save me.

I filed the thought away for later. That was going to have to be part of the conversation. Maybe the first part.

For the moment, though, I sat next to Sherman with my hands folded in my lap, scenario after scenario running through my head. Until my uncle leaned over and whispered, "Are you sure I can't interest you in helping out an old man? All I need you to do is some fire cleanup. It's just a little different from what you already do, but you'd be able to see if anything has been left behind and help out Bertie, because he really is overwhelmed. Help two old men out, Tallie. I really think I'm going to need your superior skills on this one, and now you're free to do what you want."

Buttered like I liked my toast when I was in the mood to dip it into a huge cup of Gina's awesome hot chocolate. And yet my curiosity was seriously piqued.

"Can we meet for coffee to discuss?" I whispered back. "I feel like we reached a good space here and I don't want to set things off again by worrying my parents that I'm getting involved in something I can't handle."

"Bean There, Done That at eight tomorrow?"

"You got it. I'll let Gina know we're coming in," I whispered back.

Grams clapped her hands to end any other discussion.

"Well, now that that's settled, I believe it's almost time for pie. After the girls do the dishes," Grams said, not moving an inch from her chair.

Gina and I dutifully rose from our chairs. When my mother scooted back, Grams clamped a hand on her wrist. "You can stay."

"Why don't you and Dad talk to Max?" I said, to take the sting out of her mother once again taking over.

"Thanks, Tallie."

Gina and I trooped out to the kitchen with a sigh. I had debated being there for the conversation, but thought it better to let Max initially handle it on his own. And I didn't want to leave Gina to do the dishes by herself. On my way out, I did caution Max against making any decisions or finalizing anything before he and I had a chance to sort out the details. He kissed me on the nose and told me he'd never dream of doing something without discussing it with me.

I wasn't sure at first whether he was serious or not because he'd effectively just offered himself up on the altar of family help without letting me know he'd even thought of it, but I decided to trust him for the moment and get with Gina about coffee.

"So, what do you think about Sherman's offer?" I asked as she handed me a rinsed glass for the dishwasher.

"Are you sure you don't want to talk about Max's offer first, or why your brother seems to think I'll wait forever for his offer of marriage?"

I looked at the counter full of dishes and pots galore. We'd be here for a while. "I'm pretty sure we can cover all those and still have some dishes left."

She laughed and flicked some water at me. "You always were curious, and while I get that you don't want to make a career out of this, if Sherman thinks you can help with his firebug, why not? Just be careful and pass anything to Sherman that you find, instead of hunting down the leads yourself."

"I was afraid you were going to say that." I sighed, bumping her out of the way and manning the sink. "Move over. I'll wash and you can load the dishwasher."

"I was afraid you were going to say *that*." She laughed. "If you didn't want me to give my honest opinion, you shouldn't have asked."

"No, Gina, I'm glad I did. I feel kind of weird looking into something that has nothing to do with me. But Sherman is asking, so I hate to disappoint him."

"Then don't. Just be careful. A firebug isn't going to be much different from a murderer. You've faced those before, but none of them were on a spree of doing it for the sheer pleasure of watching people die. Everyone had a secret they either wanted to keep hidden, or one they wanted out in the open. This person might just like to watch fire dance, which means they'll be far more likely to want to hide their secret instead of accidentally setting fires in a moment of passion and want to hide them."

"I'll keep it in mind. Sherman and I are going to come for coffee in the morning tomorrow at the Bean to discuss. Do you mind?"

She loaded three more glasses and snickered. "Absolutely not. I always enjoy having Sherman in. That man can eat, and he likes to leave big tips. Better than Burton anyway."

Burton. I hadn't heard from him yet, even though "we" were supposed to be finding Hoagie and, by extension, Ronda's murderer. Sherman had confirmed they hadn't found him yet, so I guess I was going to have to call Burton at some point. Or maybe I should just call the tip line and see what happened from there. Decisions, decisions.

"But first, I don't know how I feel about getting involved with Ronda's murder." I swirled some bubbles around in the sink. "She's family, but I didn't care for her much. But I love Uncle Hoagie. What if it's him, though? I don't know if I could handle that."

"Pshaw, don't even start with that. No way would Hoagie have killed that old witch, no matter how irritating and mean she could be. He's dealt with her for years. Why now?"

"That's what I said to Max."

"So you've already been talking about it?"

"Yeah, and I guess I'll talk about it again once I hear from Burton. He said we were going to find Hoagie, but then, he also told me to use the tip line. I'm not sure what to make of that."

"Do what you want. Burton can't deny that you've helped solve some pretty big cases around here and without your help, he would have been totally lost. However, if you don't want in, you don't have to."

Indecision had me swirling a dishcloth in the sudsy water in the sink. "I don't know. My curiosity is positively boiling over, but with Max here, I feel like maybe I shouldn't get involved this time and instead should just let Burton do his job without my help."

"You'll figure it out. You always do."

I wasn't sure what she meant: if I always figured things out for myself or always figured out the murder, but I let it go for the moment to concentrate on something else that was burning a hole into my brain. "Okay, then, let's talk about Jeremy and his stupidity." I rubbed my hands together and then rinsed another plate to hand to Gina.

She sighed again. "I don't think he's stupid. I get why he wants us to take our time, but I'm not getting any younger. And for a long time he kept saying we should get married so his reputation remained intact. But then he let it go when I told him it felt like he just wanted respectability, not me. And now that I'm ready, he's dragging his feet."

"Oh, that sounds like your mom talking, and I don't think I'm okay with that."

She smacked me with the towel she had draped over her shoulder. "Not fair and not accurate. Of course Mama Shirley wants me to get married, and have kids, and do all that stuff, but I want this, too. I just think Jeremy is waiting for something, and I don't know what it is. I wish I did, because I'd make it happen."

"I'm told I have a superior nose for sleuthing and a knack for eavesdropping. I also bet I could talk Max into asking him as his best friend. It's important to know who your resources are and use them to the best of your ability."

At that she laughed, but she didn't say no. Game on, then.

"Speaking of Max," she said, "how do you feel about him working with your dad?"

And now on to the big question I had kind of wanted to avoid until I talked with Max privately. But this was my best friend, and I tried not to deliberately hide anything from her.

I shrugged and told her my plan to talk with him and my thoughts on being an undertaker's significant other.

"Hey, I'm looking to do the same thing." She frowned at me.

"My God, it's like we're all sick or something." I shook my head. "My mother too!"

"Not at all, Tallie. It is useful work, and I know you like to do your part. Maybe Max just wants to do his instead of working with numbers all day."

I hadn't thought of it that way, so I let it roll around in my head as my mother came into the kitchen to see how we were doing.

"Wow, you girls are making huge progress. Do you mind if I stay out of the kitchen for a little bit longer? Max requested some coffee and snickerdoodles."

They must be at the negotiating part if Max wanted snickerdoodles. They always seemed to help him think, just like they did for me.

"Leave them out for us too," I said.

Her little smile left me snickering. "Of course, dear. Now, finish up those dishes and then I have real dessert ready. Chocolate chip cheesecake."

I stopped scrubbing altogether, my rubber-gloved

hands resting in the sink filled with hot sudsy water for the things that weren't going to go into the dishwasher. "You didn't."

"I most certainly did." Her smile went wider. "Perhaps I had this woman's intuition that we might be celebrating tonight. You're not the only one who knows things, Tallie." And with that cryptic comment, she took off with her plate of cookies and the smile still firmly on her face.

"What do think that was all about?" I asked Gina.

"I have no idea, but now I'm intrigued. Do you think you should go in to the meeting with your parents and Max? Will he decide without you? Is that what she thinks we'll be celebrating? But how would she have known?"

"He won't agree to anything without talking to me if he knows what's good for him."

"We've got two good guys, don't we?" She leaned her head on my shoulder.

We used to stand like this all the time when we were younger, dreaming and wishing for boys who would love us, make us feel like princesses, and thinking of names for children, what kind of car we'd drive, and what kind of house we'd own. Making up lives for ourselves.

And the lives we'd dreamed had turned out much different, but I wouldn't change a minute of it if it brought me right here, standing like this with my best friend in my mother's kitchen. Even if we did have another murderer in town and I was going to have to help figure out whodunit and why so we could catch them before they hurt anyone else.

"Love you," I said.

"Love you more. Now, let's get the rest of these dishes done and find out what your parents are going to offer their newest family addition. You know they're going to be even more pressing on getting the two of you married if Max turns out to be good at being a funeral director. They won't want to lose him if you decide to break up."

Lordy, that was the last thing I needed to worry about. But we were solid, and he wasn't going anywhere. Or at least I hoped not. If my dad drove him crazy enough, though, all bets might be off. Maybe we should have held off on the renovations until we saw whether Max would survive working with my father, my mother and my brother.

I followed Gina back out into the dining room, where there was indeed chocolate chip cheesecake, candles on the table and Jeremy down on one knee with a beautiful, blue-velvet box in his hands and a soft smile on his face, all for Gina.

Chapter Six

"You brat! Did you know?" I teased Max on our way out the door, loaded down with leftovers and presents, just as I'd predicted. I was so thankful to have a place to put everything, and now we had food for the next several days.

Walking toward Max's car, we stopped short when yelling erupted from the house next door. Christmas could be rough for a lot of families, but I had to smile. The McClaren clan often had eruptions, with the six kids and a dad who brooked no crap. They also liked to play board games, and that could be a special form of war when it came to that family. I had a ton of memories of them beating their dad at Monopoly by all ganging up on him and tromping him. Good times.

I let Max drive home because he was feeling a certain

amount of chivalry after watching the heart-melting way my brother had proposed to my best friend.

Jeremy had said all the right words in the right tone and with the right facial expressions, and not one moment felt false. For Gina's part, she had been on her knees with him on the floor before he got the first word out and was trying to pry the ring out of the box before he'd even asked. He kissed her instead, and it was the loveliest thing I'd seen in years. He'd done good, I'd give him that, though I wasn't going to tell him so. He had other things to take care of.

"I did know," Max said smugly, and I would have socked him in the arm if he wasn't making a turn. I didn't want him to hit the curb or get into an accident.

"I can't believe you kept it a secret from me."

"We had other things going on, and Jeremy told me he was proposing, but not exactly when. He didn't decide that until the two of you were in the kitchen. He's been carrying around the ring for weeks. Good choice; the girl and the ring." He turned just enough to wink at me.

I conceded that the ring was beautiful, square-cut and made from a ring that had been my great-grandmother's, which my mom had been holding on to for years and years. And the girl was awesome too, so I'd let this whole secret-keeping thing slide.

Just this once.

"You can have that secret without getting in trouble, but I would like to know about any others before you decide to spring things on me, like this helping-at-the-funeral-home thing. Are you really sure you want to do that?" I knotted my hands in my lap, happy I wasn't driving, but happier when we pulled into the parking lot behind the funeral home. I met Max at the back of the car to go in.

He unlocked the door and then held my hand as we went up the two flights of stairs to our new magnificent abode, even if I didn't want to live in the funeral home. I might not have a choice anymore if Max loved being a part of the family business.

"Tallie, I know you're not a huge lover of the business, but I can see the benefits and the huge satisfaction in helping those who are left behind to move through the grief. I think it will be nice to not always be on the other side of the desk from someone who is either trying to cheat on their taxes, trying to figure out how to cheat on their taxes or who has already cheated on their taxes and wants me to ignore that fact."

"I suppose. But the funeral business can be so sad." I walked up the carpeted stairs backward to keep him in sight. Running my hand over the wallpaper kept me centered and away from falling down the stairs.

"And fulfilling. I might not have been made for this from the beginning, but Jeremy knew what he wanted to be when we were in grade school together. He used to get razzed endlessly about being the guy only dead people liked. He was called Cadaver Boy for years, and yet he still does it with his whole heart. Let's put aside the sibling rivalry for a minute. Tell me what you really think about how he does his job."

"Fantastically," I said with absolutely no hesitation, standing on the landing outside our apartment door.

"Then maybe I can at least do mine well. And it's not

forever. I told your dad I would discuss it with you and
then we'd see over a trial year. If we all decide it would
be a better fit for me to go back to taxes, I won't have
been out of the game too long to slip right back in."

"You're a good man, Max Bennett." I stepped into his
arms.

"You're not so bad yourself, Tallulah Graver. Even if
you are always getting involved in these murder cases."
He rested his chin on top of my head as we stood there for
just a minute. "I was wondering if we could also take that
year to live together and see if you really want to be stuck
with me for the rest of your life before I propose marriage."

I didn't stiffen necessarily, but I went very still.
Thoughts ran through my head. Did I want to be married
again? Waldo had not been an awesome husband, but
then, I hadn't been a great wife either, so that was a draw.
My parents had a great marriage, and I knew, without a
shadow of a doubt, that Jeremy and Gina would make a
lasting marriage, but was I capable of that?

"I have to wait a whole year?" The words popped out
of my mouth without me thinking them through.

He laughed, and I felt it vibrate in my chest. "I'd propose to you right now if I thought you'd say yes, but I
don't want to go too early with you and scare you off."

"I'd say yes if you had a ring," I said cheekily.

He reached into his pocket and laughed when I backed
up a half step.

"I'm just getting out a piece of paper to write down
that you said yes, so now you can't take it back." He
turned up my face and kissed me softly. "Maybe it will be

sometime within the next year. We'll see, but you said yes. I'm going to call that a win." He smiled. "And with that, I'm going to look through my minute client list until your dad puts me on the schedule. We're going to need to speed up the progress on the apartment. We need all this space and the extra bathrooms and an actual bedroom if I have to be up at all hours to answer a call in the middle of the night and be presentable."

He kissed my knuckles and walked away.

Max. A funeral director. Well, if anyone suspicious came into the funeral parlor, I wouldn't have to ask my dad or brother for the details anymore. I could just ask Max. Always looking on the bright side of life, that was me. Me and my soon-to-be undertaker boyfriend. Oh Lordy.

I said goodbye to Max at about seven forty-five in the morning the day after Christmas. He grunted and rolled away from me. Immediately, Mr. Fleefers sat on his hip and Peanut cuddled up against his back, where I had been moments ago.

The grunting was not exactly the way I'd wanted to start out the morning, but right now he was adorable, and no matter his decision about the funeral director thing, he was mine. The rest we'd figure out as we went along.

Arriving at the Bean, I staked out a table while I waited for Uncle Sherman to show up. Soon I would be able to eat all the things. I should still be stuffed from dinner last night, but I wasn't and eyed a chocolate-chocolate chip muffin in the case at the counter with my mouth watering. I settled for a cup of whoopie pie latte and chatting with Mama Shirley while I cooled my heels.

She smiled as she came up to the table. "Glad to see your brother finally did the right thing."

"I twisted his arm, you know. Told him that he'd better do it soon or you were going to come after him with that deadly rolling pin of yours."

She paused for a second while in the act of putting down my cup. "You didn't."

I laughed. "No, I didn't. He came up with it all on his own. I'm actually superproud of him, not that I'll tell him that."

"Yeah, he doesn't need to have a swollen head on top of the magnificent catch he just made." She flipped back her platinum-blond hair with a sparkle in her eyes.

We both laughed this time as Sherman walked through the door.

"Care to share the joke? I need a laugh right about now."

Sherman looked drained. For all the laughing he did and the irreverence he showed for our police chief, he must be taking the firebug hard if he looked like he'd been run over by one of his own fire trucks.

Mama Shirley bustled away to get him a cup of whatever he usually drank. I waited for him to sit down and then took his hand.

"All joking aside, are you okay?" I asked.

"Not really, Tallie. This is wearing heavy on me. I can't seem to find him, or her, and I don't even know where to start looking. I know it's eventually going to be Burton's thing, being that arson is a crime, and it's in the fire investigator's hands right now, but I don't like someone in my town burning things. We're still combing through the fire from Christmas Eve. They're escalating, and I need to get them stopped."

"I heard the sirens going next door at one in the morning and wondered if you'd had one last night too."

Sherman waved a hand at me. "No, that was a normal fire on a stove. Why do people throw water on grease fires? Maybe I should run a class or something. Anyway, it's frustrating as anything. I feel reactive, not proactive, and I just thought if you could look around and keep your ear to the ground while helping Bertie with this enormous load, maybe I'd be able to hand Burton the bad guy like you do with those murders."

"Of course I'll help." I tapped my fingers on the tabletop with nervousness. I was going to do this, but would I help or hinder?

"Your dad's probably not going to like it a lot."

"Pssh, he can deal." That, at least, I had confidence in. "Now that he's got my boyfriend in his clutches, there's probably not a lot I can do wrong. And I'll still be doing the cleaning, just in a different kind of way, so he won't be able to yell too much."

That got a small chuckle. "I'm sure he'll still find something, being the old coot he is. I do appreciate any help you can give me, though. I'm not sure what exactly I expect you to do except just be you."

Well, that was a change of pace from the way Burton normally treated me, although lately he'd been softening when I met him in here to talk about the murder podcasts I'd been listening to. And maybe one of them would help me help Hoagie. It was worth thinking about at least.

*   *   *

I went home, where the delicious smell of something filled the air. I wasn't sure what it was, but apparently, Max had taken to that Pennsylvania Dutch cookbook and started using our kitchen as a testing ground. Maybe he was trying to distract me because he was serious about working in the funeral home and thought he needed to get me loaded up with sugar to go along with his plan.

Either way, I was fine with it, as long as it was something delicious and worth the extra pounds I might gain just by looking at it. Fortunately, Sherman and I had sat at the coffeehouse for almost an hour, shooting the breeze, so I could eat again without feeling any guilt.

I stepped into our kitchen to find Max taking a cake out of the oven. "Oh my, is that a fudge bottom cake? Please tell me it is."

His smile was wild and a little wicked. "It is. Maybe I should open a bakery instead."

"Uh, no, I refuse to have you wake up at four every morning to serve other people delicious things, and I don't think my waist could handle it."

"Ah, but this one's not for you."

I was baffled into silence. But then I found my voice. "What? Why? How?" I felt like we had already had this kind of conversation, and then I remembered that last time it was because he had decorated our house and made things beautiful. This time he appeared to be ruining my life.

"Well, it's for you, if you want to go with me to see how the investigation is going for Burton. It's his birthday, you know, and I thought it would be good community relations to give him a cake."

"Smart and yet completely underhanded. I knew there was a reason I loved you."

He laughed and wrapped me in a hug. "I'm happy I'm here."

"Me too. Now, let's go get that to Burton and see what's happening."

Chapter Seven

But when we showed up at the station, the birthday boy was nowhere to be found, and Suzy was as tight-lipped as ever, even when I explained to her that, according to Burton, "we" were trying to find Hoagie.

Max made quick work of a piece of the cake, drowning it in the hot fudge that sat under the cake itself.

Suzy smiled up at him as she took her time finishing her own cake. "He's at the hardware store."

The perfect excuse to go find him was in Max's hands, along with a carton of vanilla ice cream and a scooper. Plus, if anyone would know where Hoagie was or who might have wanted Ronda dead, it would be his sidekick for the last twenty years, Nathan Front, the guy who'd worked in the hardware store since he was sixteen and the one who'd been cranking the cage at the fire hall for bingo. He was also my crew member Jenna's husband, and I'd use that connection if necessary.

"Great, and we can get the new toilet seat while we're there, Tallie." Max smiled and I stifled a groan. I did not want to shop again.

Just awesome.

Because we had always seemed to need something more once we found another issue, we had become frequent customers of the local hardware store. Maybe that would change when we finally gave the project over to a contractor. I felt alternately like I never wanted to step foot in the store again and like I should set up a cot and at least a hot plate so I could make it my new home away from home, seeing as we were there all the time.

But the hardware store was owned by Hoagie, who, for one, was a good guy and, for two, was one of my relatives, so I had decided early on not to burn it down, no matter how much I wanted to. It was a close thing, though, in the days after we'd started the renovation. I had even found myself eyeing the gas cans and the flame throwers just to amuse myself.

I probably shouldn't even make a joke like that now I was looking into arson.

Not that I'd ever do something that destructive. My days of being a nuisance in town had ended when I'd divorced my ex-husband, Walden Phillips III, less affectionately known as Waldo.

Well, I had stopped being a nuisance to everyone except the chief of police, Burton, who thought I was always a nuisance, especially when there was a corpse to be found and a murderer to be apprehended. But maybe not this time. I was having a hard time wrapping my head around the fact that I'd been invited in this time. Although it wasn't exactly panning out the way Burton had made it sound if I had no information and was chasing him around with hot fudge cake baked by Max.

"Do we have a plan?" I asked Max as we walked down the center aisle of Hoagie Hogart's hardware store. It was a nice store, with plain shelving, filled with all manner of things that you could ever dream of to fix your house or your lawn or your garden. Right now, it was also packed with shovels and rock salt to deal with the snow that had fallen this winter.

We took a left into the paint aisle before Max answered.

"Not really. Before we leave, I'd like to get into my office here, but first I was thinking we just should find Burton and thank him for all he does."

"That sounds shady."

"Like a big old oak tree in the forest."

I rolled my eyes at him. "I know you're trying to be funny, but it's not working at the moment."

"Already getting sick of me? I've only been here for a few months."

I bumped my shoulder into his arm. "I'm not sick of you at all, and you know it. It's more that if you're going to live in town, you have to get to know the players, and Burton is one of those people you stay under the radar with if you don't want to have a run-in with negativity over and over again when he's in a snit."

"Ah, I've got you now. So, you're warning me off him in case I might get my feelings hurt. I have been around enough to know how he reacts to people."

"You are impossible. Do what you want, but don't

come running to me for snickerdoodles if he starts swearing at you and telling you that you should mind your own business because you're an imbecile."

Max shook his head. "He wouldn't. He's a cop and must know the virtues of being nice to the people who actually bring things to you to help solve the case."

I scoffed. "You just said you've been around enough to know how he reacts and then you pop off with that? Have you not been around for all the other ones? Maybe he was just being nice Christmas Eve at bingo, but he's probably going to get all up in arms any moment now. I know him. But this is the best place to look for Hoagie, so I'm with you, and your cake and ice cream. If anyone knows where Hoagie is, or who killed Ronda, it might just be Nathan, not Burton. The only person she was even remotely nice to when she was in a mood was Nathan, and that's only because the guy has worked here since he was a teenager, to help out his family, and Ronda knew she couldn't get rid of him without seriously irritating Hoagie."

Or maybe that was what had happened. Maybe Ronda had tried to get rid of Nathan and it had irritated Hoagie enough to force his hand and varnish can? It could also explain Ronda's interaction with Nathan's wife, Jenna. At least it could if I contorted it right.

Although I still didn't want to believe that Hoagie had been pushed to the point where he'd take a life instead of just divorcing his wife.

"Not that she hadn't tried to get rid of me a few times over the years," Nathan said, meeting us at the end of the aisle.

I flushed. I had hoped no one would hear me over the churning of mixing paints and the loud talk between two men about nail sizes and which plunger worked best when trying to clean out a clogged toilet. I could have told them that from my experience as a cleaner, but no one had asked me.

"Hey, Nathan." I played it off like nothing had happened because I didn't want to embarrass him or myself any more than I already had.

"It's okay, Tallie. Ronda could be a bit much sometimes, but she was a good woman underneath that gruff. Maybe like the Grinch."

"Who hadn't yet learned that her heart is three times too small?" Oh, maybe I shouldn't have said that.

But Nathan laughed. "She'll be missed terribly." He stretched out his hand to Max, who took it and shook it. "Good to see you, Max. Are you back for more supplies? I thought the house was almost done."

"It is, but I was looking for Burton."

"That must be the reason for the picnic basket on your arm."

Max blushed a little, being that the basket was decked out in checks and festooned with balloons. He'd gone all-out. But now I thought he might be rethinking the offering to the God of the police station and making it look so froufrou.

"Actually, I was wondering if you might be able to help me find a new varnish for a piece of furniture I'm refinishing."

Not quite the save he probably wanted to go with, but it at least distracted Nathan from checking out the basket again. He walked to the shelf and pulled down a can marked with Hoagie's personalized stamp, which he put on everything. A hammer with a smiley face on the head and the Mr. Yuk sticker.

It reminded me of the can I'd seen next to Ronda's head. How had it gotten there, and who had put it there? Why would the killer have left it behind? Was it really what she'd been killed with? That had to have hurt before she had faded out. And would have necessitated quite a bit of anger, I'd think. I was going to ask about recent purchases by anyone who had hated Ronda, but then Nathan and Max were lost in the wonders of chemicals and compounds, shine and durability.

I wandered off because my mission today, whether or not I chose to accept it, was to find a new toilet seat for the original bathroom. I didn't want to have to be here any longer than absolutely necessary, so I figured I should start now. Especially if Burton wasn't here. Nathan hadn't answered Max's question, so I figured he'd probably already headed out to his next stop.

Plus the only chemicals I knew were the ones you cleaned with, and I was happy in not expanding that knowledge.

Not that I was thrilled to be looking at toilet seats.

But new varnish was low on the list. Right behind buying toilet seats that would be nice and comfy but not showy. I never thought I'd be doing this. Even when Waldo had agreed to build a house, I was completely not involved in the construction or picking anything out. Waldo had handled all that. I'd bought a few things for the house and decorated it a time or two, but the basic stuff had not been my forte. And I was pretty sure it wasn't now either.

Yet now we had put in a full-size bath and a half-bath in the new section and left the one small bathroom that had been there for years as it was. That meant a new toilet seat, because the other two toilets were brand-new and Max wanted them all to look new. That's how I found myself staring at a wall of toilet seats and trying to find any enthusiasm whatsoever.

I still hadn't found it when Max came around the corner with a big smile on his face. "I have the varnish. Did you pick a toilet seat?"

"Of course," I said, grabbing one that looked similar to the others off the wall. "All nice and cushy and not showy. Just like you asked for." I looked down at the product in my hands and breathed a sigh of relief that I hadn't accidentally grabbed the blue one.

"We're ready to check out, then. If you want to take the things home, I can stop in the office."

"I thought you were going to get me access to look around up there, too."

"Maybe not now, Tallie," he said in a low voice. "Nathan's a little overwhelmed with all this, and it might be better to come back in a few hours." Then he raised his voice. "We need to drop off this cake to Burton anyway."

I followed him to the front counter, where Nathan stood with a line at his register and not a single other person dressed in the familiar gray shirt anywhere in sight. And still no Burton.

Ten minutes later, no one had shown up to help Nathan. I glanced up at the office on the second floor where Hoagie had an office and the staff had a break room. The blinds twitched closed, but no one emerged.

Finally, it was our turn. "Nathan, don't you think you should call for help?" I looked behind me and there were six other people in line, looking out around the crowd to see how much longer it was going to be. Some had huge buckets of tools; others were scooting big buckets of plaster across the floor a foot at a time. Then you had the ones who should have grabbed a cart at the front of the store and instead decided to pick up just one or seven more things and were loaded down to the point that they couldn't see over their load of all things hardware. Ah, everyone loved an after-Christmas sale.

"It's fine, Tallie." He said it with his usual smile, but there was strain around the edges. "I don't have anyone willing to come in today and the kids are all looking for their dad."

"Come on, Nathan, someone should be down here helping you. They can't all be looking for him and leaving you here to work this all by yourself. Why didn't you close today?"

He rang up the toilet seat before he looked up and answered me, his face serious along with his voice. "Because he helped, Tallie, and someday I'll be able to help just like he did." And then the smile was back, as if the moment of seriousness had not happened. "Toilet seats were on sale today. This one was half off. That's a really good deal."

I frowned at him as Max took the plastic bags Nathan handed over the counter. "You deserve better."

"Tallie, I have everything I could ever want, and more coming soon. Don't you worry about me. I've got this in the bag." And he lifted up the bag full of more supplies, chuckling when I deepened my frown.

Max handed over the credit card we'd gotten to pay for all house repairs so that we could keep track of our expenses. Nathan ran the card, still smiling peacefully when a shout rang out across the store, amplified by the bare ceiling. The whole line looked over our shoulders to the second floor. Something smashed up against the venetian blinds, closed on the big window upstairs, flattening the white slats. What on earth was going on up there?

Had someone fallen? Were they in trouble? Why was anyone up there at all when Nathan had said no one had come in today?

There was another shout, and then the fire alarms blared. Then the sprinklers creaked open and spray shot out over the entire store. I found myself being shielded by a toilet seat in a plastic bag as Max and I made a mad dash for the exit.

Chapter Eight

The hardware store was less than three blocks from the fire station, so Uncle Sherman and his crew were at the store within minutes. They responded to all emergencies, volunteers geared up for anything, no matter the size of the fire.

And this one couldn't have been that big because I hadn't even smelled a whiff of smoke before the sprinklers went on.

We were all herded across the pavement to the opposite side of Main Street. Traffic stopped for the trucks to pull up in the parking lot next to the store, and then it was like a well-choreographed ballet.

Sherman directed like a drill sergeant, but most of the volunteers were already moving in the right direction before he even gave out any orders. The hoses were pulled from the reels, ladders were extended and the fire itself was assessed.

And what a fire it was. But curiously, it was next door at the chocolatier, not at the actual hardware store. Maybe that was why I hadn't smelled any smoke when the fire alarms in the store went off. The buildings weren't connected, so their alarms wouldn't have been hooked up into each other. Not that I knew of. The danger was real that the fire could jump from building to building. Most of the buildings were built so close together that you couldn't walk between them without turning sideways. Maybe the alarms for the two businesses were hooked together, just as a precaution.

And the threat was very real—in the ten minutes we'd been outside, the entire back of the cinder-block building had gone up in flames. It was mesmerizing to watch them lick up the side of the exterior wall and dance across the roof. It was also terrifying because I couldn't seem to find Nathan in the gathering crowd.

"Do you see Nathan?" I asked Max in a low voice. I didn't want to set anyone off if I had just missed him with all the people standing on the sidewalk—far more than had been in the store with us. But a fire was a big event in our tiny town in Central Pennsylvania, especially when it was Main Street in the middle of the afternoon.

"I haven't, but I'm sure he's somewhere, probably talking to Sherman."

But Sherman came into view, and he was walking alone until the chief of police and my former nemesis, Burton, joined him on the sidewalk. I ducked behind Max instinctively. Apparently, it was still a habit not to want to catch his attention.

"Tallie, you're being ridiculous. He's been nice to you for months and didn't yell at you when you found Ronda. You need to trust that it's not going to go back to the way it was."

"I'd like to trust that, but he's turned on me before, and if anyone got left behind in the building, I don't want to be the person he is looking at." I remembered my thought that I'd considered setting the place on fire just to get rid of it and was so thankful I'd never said it out loud. I couldn't even imagine what a field day Burton would have had with that.

"It's going to be fine. It looks like everyone got out."

I looked around the crowd again and spotted Nathan, looking shaken and slightly green. I had been the last person to talk to him in the store, so I thought it only right that I go talk with him now to make sure he was okay. Or at least that was the story I told myself when I couldn't contain my curiosity anymore.

"Hey, Nathan, you okay?" I said as Max trailed behind me. We met Nathan at the curb. Up close, he looked like death warmed over instead of just slightly green.

"I . . . I . . . I can't find Hoagie. He's not anywhere and I can't find him, and I have to find him and I can't find him." He shook his head, as if trying to clear an image from it. Closing his eyes, he slapped a hand to his forehead. I was very much afraid that he was about to throw up. While I was capable of many things, helping someone who was puking was certainly not one of them.

Catching one of the EMTs by the arm as he walked by, I prepared to hand Nathan over to him. And then I realized it was Ray, the one who always liked to make fun of me.

"No dead body this time, Tallie. I'm both impressed and a little disappointed."

I made a cutting motion at my throat, but he either didn't see it or willfully chose to ignore it. Either way, he kept on talking.

"Burton will be pleased, though."

Max cut in. "Ray, not now. Why don't you see if Nathan needs any help? He looks like he might be nauseous."

That stopped the EMT in his tracks as he looked around and finally saw Nathan between Max and me.

Nathan shook his head. "I'm fine, Tallie. Really, Ray, I'm fine. I'm going to walk home until Sherman or Burton needs me."

His footsteps dragged, and Max and I shared a look, then took up posts on either side of him.

"Let us at least make sure you get there, Nathan," I said. Nathan shook his head again, and Max took over while I kept up as best I could.

"Everything is going to be fine. Sherman is going to be able to get the fires out and then they'll be able to get the store back up and running in no time. They'll figure out what happened and make it right."

Nathan shrugged his shoulders this time, but still trudged along with us. I looked around as we made our way down the sidewalk and around the corner to Nathan's apartment above the pizza shop. Nathan looked up the metal stairs rising to his third-floor apartment. Then he dropped his head and his shoulders.

"Do you need us to go up with you?" I asked. "I know you must have a ton of stuff going through your head right now, and we're more than happy to get you settled before we go. Do you know how to get in touch with Hoagie to let him know the store is okay?" I won't lie that I slipped that in there to see if he knew where the other man was. He'd said he needed to find Hoagie as if he'd been in the store. Had he, or was Nathan so conditioned to defer to him that he automatically thought of him even though no one had seen him since Christmas Eve?

"No, that's okay. I'll be fine. I have to go make a list of all the things I need to do. I haven't seen Hoagie since anyone else has, Tallie. I wish I had, though. I need authorization to do everything. I can't make these decisions myself. Though I guess I'd better at least call Bertie over at the cleaners to see who I should talk to about getting us dried out." He took out his phone and started making notes. "It's okay, guys. I'll be better thinking about going forward instead of worrying about what just happened. I do appreciate you walking me home, but I've got it from here."

He began the long climb on the outside stairs with the switchback to his apartment. Nathan and I had gone to high school together, and I remembered him from back in the day, but we'd never really been friends. Now I wished I knew who he was friends with besides Hoagie so I could call someone over for him. But I didn't know him well enough to ask, and he probably wasn't going to tell me. I did send a quick text to Jenna, though, to let her know what had happened. Per the calendar in my phone, she was at a job but should almost be done.

Max and I were still standing at the bottom of the stairs when Nathan rounded the corner to walk up the next flight. He staggered back on the landing and slapped a hand on his mouth.

"Are you okay, Nathan?" That was Max this time, because I'd started walking toward whatever Nathan was pointing at from the second story. I knew I shouldn't. I knew it, but I couldn't seem to help myself.

Because sure enough, there was a dead body on the gravel up against the hardware store.

Unfortunately, my first thought was that at least I hadn't been the one to find it this time.

My second thought was that Burton wouldn't have to look for Hoagie anymore, but would be just as heartbroken as everyone in town that he was dead.

I ran the last few steps.

"I'm going to check to see if he has a pulse." I was almost positive the answer was going to be no, but I did it anyway. Bending down, my suspicions were confirmed.

My heart clenched. Hoagie was dead on the ground in front of me. My uncle, who had been part of my growing-up years. He'd given me a job to get out of the funeral home when I was a teenager and my dad was trying to teach me the ropes with dead people. I knew I had only run just down the street, but the hardware store had been far enough away not to have to deal with funerals during my sophomore summer, when I had simply wanted to

enjoy myself and whoever I had been trying to get to notice me that year.

And Nathan had been there to teach me the ropes,
along with Hoagie. That gave me pause; then I glanced
up, and Nathan was no longer green but sheet white. Oh,
I was going to have to send Max up the stairs to bring the
poor man down. He was still standing against the railing
on the landing with his hand over his mouth. His whole
world had just fallen apart in the last half hour; I couldn't
blame him. I hoped Jenna got here soon.

"Can you go get Nathan? I think he'll need to be here,"
I said to Max, who stood slightly to my left and behind
me.

"He's really dead, then?"

Max sounded as sad as I felt. "Yeah; who knows why,
though. I don't see any damage, but it could have been
smoke inhalation. Maybe he was trying to get out the
back way and collapsed once he made it through the
door." I looked around, still crouching. The back door
was to my left and a window was right beyond that. I remembered that the door led into a storeroom, or at least
it had all those years ago when I'd worked there. It was
possible Hoagie had moved things around, but I highly
doubted it. He had always been a creature of habit.

That, however, would be a question that my not-always-
friendly chief of police would undoubtedly answer. "I
guess we're going to have to call Burton."

"I'll do it so you don't have to." Max pulled his phone
from his pocket.

I looked around the area to see if there was anything
that could have hurt Hoagie. I was careful not to touch

anything, but for some reason the whole scene looked off. Had Hoagie died in the fire or while we were in the store? But this entrance was on the opposite side of the building from where the fire had erupted in the building next door.

The blinds had flickered upstairs when we were in line, but I wouldn't have been able to tell you if it had been Hoagie. It could have been someone who was checking to make sure he, or she, could drag the body down the stairs before setting the place next door ablaze to cause a distraction. And there had been the yell and someone shoved up against the blinds. Or had someone fallen against them without being pushed? How did this all connect to Ronda being dead? Why this couple? And why now?

I was fully aware I might be making something out of nothing, but I also knew that Sherman had been chasing a firebug over the last few weeks and was getting pressure from the town to get things settled and the person caught.

So, could the firebug have moved from residences to stores? Who was it? What had they done? Or was this truly an accident? Maybe the wiring in Hoagie's store was not up to code and something had blown. Like the shoemaker's kids who had no shoes, had Hoagie spent so much time helping everyone else with their projects that he'd let things go at the hardware store?

I was having a hard time believing that. I set Hoagie's hand back on his lap and he fell over to the right. Instinctively, I reached out to grab his shoulder to keep him from hitting his head even though it was ridiculous. I encountered something and realized there was a screwdriver stuck in his back. You didn't get that by running out of a door. And on closer inspection, the corpse resembled

Hoagie, but the nose was wrong, the mole above his eye was missing, and the chin was slightly off. Being as careful as possible, I opened one eye and found a blue iris instead of the deep brown of Hoagie's eyes.

I grabbed Max's arm. "Tell Suzy in dispatch that we have a murder and it's not Hoagie, but someone who looks a lot like him."

Chapter Nine

Max tried to hand the phone to me once he'd made contact with Suzy. I didn't want it because I was trying to figure out who this was. I actively shoved the thing away in my hardened concentration.

"No, no, no. I'm not talking to anyone at the moment. Handle it and get someone over here now." I could hear Suzy squawking on the line through Max's high-end phone, but whatever she said was lost in my continued denial of the phone.

Max finally put it back up to his ear. "She won't talk. She thought it was Hoagie, but now she's saying it's not. I believe her, though the resemblance is uncanny. Nathan is the one who found him, but Tallie checked for a pulse, and it's not there."

There was more squawking. I felt bad for a half second

for leaving Max to Suzy by himself, and then I shut it down. Every other time, from Darla, my former employer, to Waldo, my ex-husband, to the woman I'd found rolled in a carpet, each death had been a body I had found, people I had then stood up for and done the dirty work to find the killer before they could do it again or get away altogether. But each time I'd known them, even Ronda, who I was willing to ask the tough questions for. Not that I'd had much of a chance to ask any questions with Hoagie missing and Sherman asking for my help. This person I did not know from Adam, or Hoagie, almost, as the case seemed to be.

And then I shook my head at myself when Burton came steaming around the corner of the hardware store and made a beeline for me. Max was on the phone, so Burton didn't even stop to tap him on the shoulder. He just came right to me, shaking his head.

"Did you hear or see anything?" he asked as he too crouched down to feel for a pulse. He shook his head again when he didn't find one and then looked up at the sky and closed his eyes. "This is bad."

"Worse than the others? Or just bad?"

"Both. What happened? Was he alive when you found him?"

I didn't know if Burton was hoping it was a heart attack or smoke inhalation, as I had thought previously, until I remembered that the hardware store hadn't been on fire but the store next to it. I hated to burst his bubble, but there was no help for it. "He's been screwdrivered." I said it solemnly, because it seemed to deserve a moment of silence. If I'd have had to say that about Hoagie, I felt like it would have been worse. To be killed with your own most useful tool in the business would be the height of irony. Like if someone came after me with a vacuum cleaner or tried to embalm my father while he was still alive.

But this was not Hoagie, and I had to keep telling myself that because the resemblance was astounding.

Burton stuck his hands on his hips with his one hand firmly gripping his gun and shook his head for a third time. He was going to injure his brain if he didn't stop that. "What is this town coming to? There is too much going on for how small and quaint we're supposed to be."

"It's still the real world, though, and these things happen in smaller towns than ours. There was a murder in a town of less than three hundred not even two years ago."

"Listening to those podcasts of yours again?"

I'd been hooked recently on listening to and watching those podcasts and television shows that dive into the evilest women, or evilest people, or small-town murder mysteries. I couldn't help myself and had taken to talking shop with Burton when I'd find him in the Bean There, Done That.

I shrugged and then bit my lip and nodded.

"Well, I hope you're ready for this one, because I have no idea who this guy is, but at first glance I would have definitely thought it was Hoagie." Burton scratched his head. "I just don't know what to think. Is someone going after the Hogarts? Do I need to warn their kids? It can't be a coincidence that it was Ronda and now it's a Hoagie look-alike. Was whoever did this trying to cover it up and hoping that the fire would catch and burn this one beyond recognition?"

I felt Burton was more talking to himself than actually asking my opinion, so I held my tongue. I didn't have any theories or anything solid to add anyway, but this way I'd get points for not trying to insert my opinions where they might not be wanted in the first place.

Then I looked around at the way the pseudo-Hoagie slumped on his side, with his silvered and sparse hair flopped over his forehead. He'd been beaned with something too; he had a dent in his head and his eyes were vacant.

He was dressed just like Hoagie and had a familiar look on his face. That smile that seemed to be there no matter what was going on. But how could he have been smiling when he got hit in the head with something hard enough to not only hurt him but also kill him? Wouldn't he have at least been grimacing? I touched the laugh lines on either side of his mouth and snatched my hand back quickly.

"Um, Burton?"

"What, Tallie? I'm trying to think what to do from here. I have a missing person, two dead people, one of them a look-alike for the guy I want to find and can't and fires being set all over the place. What could you possibly need?"

I clamped my lips shut, then took in a breath through my nose. Now was not the time to smart off to him. No matter how much I wanted to.

"I just wanted to point out that this guy is very cold,

like not newly dead cold, not even cold over a period of a few hours. He has a cast to his eyes and his jaw has been wired shut. In my not-so-expert opinion, I think you're going to find that he's been embalmed and has been dead for long enough to have that done."

Who knew Burton could gasp like that without fainting? And who knew that my job as a funeral assistant might one day put me in this position?

We stood around for ten minutes while my father was called to check out the corpse. I urged Max to hand over the cake he'd made for Burton's birthday to pass the time. It was a little sodden and maybe not as good as it would have been fresh, but it did get a nod from Burton and a small smile.

I had not wanted to have my father called, but didn't think calling Jeremy instead would have been any better. And my dad was an old hand at this. He would be the best one to check out for any other signs that this person was dead and had been dead long enough to have gone through the whole funeral preparation process.

Burton and I didn't talk much during those ten minutes. Max went up to get Nathan and ask him to come down just in case he needed to be questioned. But we all kind of stood around looking at one another with quick glances but not saying anything.

I actually breathed a sigh of relief when my father walked up at a brisk pace and drew to a halt in front of Burton. "What's the situation? Usually I'm called in much later than this. If you need me to talk to Tallie about staying out of your business, I think we all know that's fruitless."

Ah, good old Dad did not come to the rescue. It didn't matter, though. He would find out soon enough what this was all about. Then he'd start hemming and hawing and making excuses instead of actually apologizing, because that's what he did. Fortunately, it didn't bother me, because I knew what I had and hadn't done and was perfectly comfortable watching him stutter over himself as soon as he figured out he'd been a jerk.

So I leaned back against the wall, just waiting.

Burton shook his head and sighed too. "Bud, I need you to tell me if this corpse has been embalmed."

"What?" Dad crouched down in front of the pseudo-Hoagie. "It's Hoagie; I have his contract. And he was just seen two days ago, so I don't think anyone had time to prepare him for the casket."

"Look closer, Dad; it's not Hoagie. He's missing that mole up by his eye, and the face is just a little off."

Bud Graver's eyes flicked to mine for a brief moment and I saw the flash of guilt. It was enough.

"To tell you definitively, I'd have to take him back to the home." He lifted an eyelid and touched his jaw. "Even if he hasn't actually been embalmed, though, he has been dead for at least a few days. Long enough to fill in a few spots on his face and plump up his cheeks, as well as keep his jaw shut."

"Good work there, Tallie." Burton said the words as if they might burn his tongue.

Then again, he was smiling at me, so maybe I was just so conditioned to expecting him to be against me that I was having trouble realizing he might actually be with me. Max's words about trusting Burton popped into my head before I could open my mouth. And instead of saying anything that could have come across as snarky, I simply nodded at him.

"Tallie?" Dad looked me over.

"I felt the wires in the jaw and told Burton he should call you before he did anything else because this wasn't Hoagie. Whoever it was has been dead for a few days. Nothing much." I shrugged and went to walk away.

"Let's leave that for the moment." Dad turned to Burton. "Do you want me to have the body brought to the home and then I can tell you for certain what's been done?"

"I have no flipping idea, Bud. No flipping idea what to do at this point at all." Burton shook his head. "Can you tell me one thing? Was he hit in the head before or after he died?"

I could answer that one. "After; no blood át all. Whatever hit him cut his skin, but no blood whatsoever. Whoever did this must have gotten the body from a funeral home, then hit him on the head and put him out here for someone to find."

Now everyone was looking at me. I shrugged. "It's the only thing that makes sense. But how did they find someone who looked this much like Hoagie? Or did they think it was Hoagie? If they did, why at all?"

"Lots of questions and not a lot of answers." Burton paced away and then came back with a frown on his face. "I think we're going to have to take him to the home, Bud. This is all kinds of strange, and I'd like to have as many facts with me as possible before I do anything else. Will you have to do further damage to get the answers?"

Dad looked off into the distance. "No. There are a few things I'll have to do, but I'll be careful."

"And what are you going to do while your father works on this part of the puzzle?" Burton asked me.

An idea hit me like a bolt of lightning and I smiled. "I'm going to call around regarding a missing corpse as an official Graver Funeral Home assistant."

He nodded. "Let me know what you find out, and if you hear anything about the actual Hoagie. I really want to talk to him now. We also can't forget Ronda. Someone is out killing people or setting up staged pseudo-murders. This can't continue."

Nathan flinched, and I just caught it out of the corner of my eye. Why? I'd put Max on talking to him to see what we came up with collectively. In the meantime, I had research to do, facts to check and calls to make.

Chances were, someone would say something near me like they always did. I often thought I either had a tattoo on my forehead that said, "talk to me," or I was so invisible that no one realized I was around when they were divulging their secrets. Either way, I'd been able to help Burton a number of times with recent cases. We hadn't had one since he and I had started talking at the coffee shop about those podcasts I listened to like a junkie, so I'd be interested to see how this worked, now that we were on more friendly terms.

I stayed long enough for Jeremy to come over with the body transport van. The EMTs were no longer needed, but they took their time loading up their gear, patting the dead man's arm and shaking their heads.

What the heck was going on? Hoagie had been a standard in this town for as long as I could remember. He was a town fixture, and everyone knew him and loved him for the generous and fun guy he was. Maybe we'd all been wrong, but I was having a hard time wrapping my head around that. But who else would have done this and why?

Jeremy pulled away from the back of the hardware store with my dad in the front seat, apparently ready to do what he did best. And now it was time for me to do the same thing.

"I can practically see all the little gears in your mind switching on and steam coming out of your ears." Burton looked up from his little notebook with his face solemn.

I bit my lip. "I was just thinking that this time I can legitimately help, and do it in a way that won't make you angry with me."

Burton sighed again, and I felt like we might need to teach him to breathe normally again after this was all over. "I was never mad at you."

I snorted.

"Okay, yes," he admitted, "I wanted you to butt out and leave me to do my job, but many concerned citizens have given us tips throughout many investigations. It was never the info you gave me. It was how you got it, and how you went about giving it to me. Look, if you think you can find out where that body came from, and why it looks so much like our missing Hoagie, I'm certainly not going to turn you away. But don't take too many risks, and don't go getting yourself in trouble."

"I can't make any promises."

"Yeah, well, I'm used to that, so I'm not holding my breath, but two bodies in three days and another two fires means that we have got to get this thing figured out. If you can help, then, honestly, I'm not going to turn you away this time. Bring it on."

Well, then, an official invitation. I wasn't sure if I really wanted to do this, but it looked like I was at least going to be involved in this particular part. At least I didn't have to be in the basement with my dad and Jeremy, pulling apart a man who was already dead—and one we didn't know.

Chapter Ten

Digging the directory out of the bottom drawer of the rarely used desk in the second-floor office of the funeral home, I bit my lip as I tried to come up with a game plan. I couldn't exactly call up every local funeral home to ask if they were missing a body.

But what to do first? I tapped the eraser of my number two pencil on the blotter atop the desk, wishing inspiration would come to me.

I pushed the chair back from the desk and spun around in it, thinking that maybe scrambling my brain might help.

And surprisingly, it did. I ground to a halt facing the back wall and saw the funeral director league of extraordinary people. Well, it was actually an association, like the bar association for lawyers or the screen actors guild. But would they be open the day after Christmas? It couldn't hurt to try. I was having a hard time believing it was only the twenty-sixth because so much had happened between opening presents and now.

Placing a call to the National Funeral Directors Association, I waited for the answering service to pick up and got a person instead.

"Oh, uh, hi." That was not quite how I wanted to start the conversation, but the woman had caught me off guard.

"Yes, what can I do for you?" the woman on the line said impatiently.

I really should have planned better for this before pressing the numbers. Dang it!

"Uh, I have a strange question."

"Doesn't everyone."

"It has to do with dead bodies." I sounded dumber with each thing I uttered, so I took a deep breath and prepared to start again.

The woman sighed. "Look, I've had it up to here today with weird requests. All the crazies seem to be finding our number fascinating. So if you want to know about necrophilia, or how to dissolve a corpse, then there must be a full moon because I have fielded twenty questions like that since this morning. Go ahead and hang up, because I'm not telling you anything. Look it up on the internet if you're that fascinated with death. I don't have time. Bye."

"Wait! Don't hang up, please."

Another sigh shot over the line. What was it with me eliciting sighs today? "At least wow me with the idiocy of your question."

I paused, but not for long. I didn't want her to think I'd hung up. "Hmm, I could come up with something that would knock you back on your heels, but instead I'd like to start over. I apologize for not introducing myself. I was expecting to get the answering service because it's the holiday week. My name is Tallie Graver, and I'm part of Graver Funeral Home in Pennsylvania."

Nothing; no sigh, no groan. But then she squeaked and cleared her throat. "Ms. Graver, my deepest apologies for my earlier words. It has been quite the day already, but that's no excuse for my insolence and ignorant remarks to you." I heard clicking and wondered if she was writing an email or searching for our website to see who she was dealing with.

I could tell her that without her having to do the dirty work.

"No need to apologize, and it's not that big a deal. I'm sure you get some real crazies calling. I admire your ability to do your job and would probably have done the same thing. In fact, I once had someone call about how to effectively dig up a grave so they could take the jewelry from the corpse. I told her that the only way the person wouldn't haunt her was if she used a teaspoon to remove the six feet of dirt. If she used a shovel, she would be visited nightly for the rest of her life."

A burst of laughter was a step in the right direction. "And did she listen to you?"

"I doubt it. My cousin never takes my advice, and it's very much to her detriment."

Another laugh. "Oh, I needed that. Thank you, and I am sorry about how I answered the phone. Thanks for understanding."

"No worries. We all have crappy days. I won't take up much more of yours, though. I was wondering if there's been any kind of bulletin about a missing body in the state. We found a male leaned up against a wall and he was not someone we had taken care of, so we're wondering if perhaps another funeral home reported a case of a missing person?" Or should I have said body? I wasn't sure what the right terminology for this particular situation was.

"Missing person, as in someone missing a body at a funeral home?" More tapping. "I'm checking now, but that's not something we normally hear about." More tapping had me waiting patiently because I didn't want to interrupt her concentration. I really, really hoped she was going to come back with something useful.

"Interesting. I do see something here; let me read it. Can I put you on hold?"

I would rather she didn't, but I couldn't exactly say that when she was helping me.

I agreed and then listened to Muzak for a while. Christmas carols played through the line. Some I knew right off and some the arrangement was so weird that I didn't know what it was until it came to the chorus. I hummed along to the ones I vaguely recognized and sang the ones I knew the words for. I was in mid-"Winter Wonderland" when she came back on.

"Oh, that's one of my favorite songs. Are they still playing those?"

Thankfully, she couldn't see me flush. "Ah, yes."

"I really like the one by Annie Lennox."

"Oh, me too."

"Don't get me started on all those reboots of 'Last Christmas,' though; no one does it like George Michael."

"I'm with you on that. He did the best."

She laughed. "But you didn't call to talk Christmas music. I had to look you up on the computer to make sure

I wasn't giving information to someone who wasn't attached to a funeral home. I see that you're with your father?"

Thank goodness he had put me on the website, although I guess I could have just pulled a name from anywhere and given it to her. I wasn't going to bring that up, though, if she didn't have a mind that constantly doubted what she was told.

"Yes, I have been for a couple of years now."

"Had you always wanted to follow in his footsteps?"

Absolutely not, and that was not why I'd called, but I needed to humor her if I wanted that information. "I work there part-time and also clean houses."

"A little variety is the spice of life. I couldn't imagine working with the dead all the time. I much prefer paperwork." She paused, but I didn't hear any clicking this time, so I wasn't sure what the holdup was. "Anyway, sorry, I didn't mean to talk your ear off."

"No, it's okay. Were you able to find anything?"

"Yes, in the bulletin news, we have someone from West Virginia who had a corpse as of the day before Christmas and now it's missing. The building was locked. He's frantic to find it because the family is well-connected with the horse set and he's just starting out. He doesn't want to have his reputation ruined before he gets started and would appreciate any info anyone could give him."

My heart beat faster. "Can you give me his info so I can call to see if this is the right guy?"

"Of course." She rattled off a phone number and his name, along with his website.

"I can't thank you enough," I said.

"Please, you cut my crappy day in half. I should be

thanking you. I think I might turn the phones onto the answering service and take myself out for lunch."

"If you can get a cheesesteak, I would highly recommend it."

"Honey, this is Georgia. I'm going for barbecue."

I laughed. "Enjoy, then, and thanks again"

"My pleasure. Good luck with everything."

Why did I feel like I might need it?

Once I disconnected, I wrote out a list of questions for this next call so I didn't get caught off guard like before. I had to be honest with myself, though: I wasn't sure exactly how to ask about a missing body without sounding suspicious. I'd just hope that something would come to me. Not that it had ever worked out well for me by doing that before, but hey, there could always be a first time.

The phone rang six times, and I was sure I was going to get voice mail this time, but then a man who sounded out of breath gasped a hello.

"Hi, this is Tallie Graver from Graver Funeral Home in Pennsylvania."

"Okay. I run my own funeral home, so I don't think I need whatever you might be selling. And I have a body that just fell off the table, so I should go."

"Wait, I have a question about the body that's missing from your home."

"Oh God, not another one. I should never have posted that on the bulletin board. Look, I don't know what happened to it and, quite frankly, with the widow missing now, and not paying for the funeral, or the embalming, I can't be bothered. And I have to get this body off the floor. His jaw just fell off."

Let him go or ask for a name? I decided to go for it because this guy did not sound like he was qualified to do anything really. "Can you at least tell me who is missing?"

"Jerry Howard. Seventy. Dead of natural causes. Wife is Wanda, and I don't know where she is either, though at least she wasn't in my care. I had to fire three people this week, and everyone keeps dying. Now can I go? The hose just slipped out and is starting to whip around the room, and I'm getting sprayed standing here."

I gulped. "Sure. Thanks for the information, I guess."

"Yeah, well, don't call back unless you have someone who knows what they're doing to share with me. I have my hands full. Literally." He grunted, and then the connection went dead.

I didn't need the vivid picture in my mind of what all he'd said was going on. I valued my father and my brother very much for a moment, because as far as I knew, we'd never had anything like that happen. Of course there were accidents, but a body falling off the table? A hose running rampant? Another missing body? What was this guy doing and how did he ever get a license?

Right now, that was not my concern. It was finding Jerry Howard and seeing if it was the same man as the one my father currently had in the basement. Once I did that, I had to find out why he looked so much like Hoagie and why he was here instead of in West Virginia. And perhaps, with all that information, it would also help me start to look into Ronda's murder. I felt like she was getting left on the back burner, but with everything that was going on, I only had so much time. I would get to her once I did all the other tasks on my to-do list.

A tall order, but one I was sure I could fill if I could just get a few snickerdoodles and talk with Gina to run a few things by her. I went out while my computer did a bunch of updates I didn't understand or care about as long as it was working when I came back.

I expected big things. Once I was properly nourished of course.

Chapter Eleven

Of course running anything by Gina was mainly an excuse to get a whoopee pie latte to go along with the snickerdoodles I planned to snatch once I got back home.

"Do we know anyone named Howard?" I asked after I'd been served a to-go cup. Gina didn't look happy about me not hanging out, but I had things to do and she did too judging from the big crowd in the café. Mama Shirley was handling gift cards with the precision of a soldier while I stole Gina for just a moment.

"First name or last?" she asked, wiping the same spot on the counter over and over again, just in case her mom looked over.

"Last name. I have a lead on something, but I need to know if we have any Howards in town."

She looked at the ceiling as if the tiles up there might

answer her question. "Not that I know of. There are Howards in Harrisburg, but I don't know of anyone here in town."

"Okay." I got up from my seat.

"Wait, you can't leave it like that. Why do you ask?"

"I don't want to talk about it too much until I know more. But has your mom filled you in on what happened earlier?" I asked Gina.

"She mentioned the fire down the street and the fact that there was a body. I was waiting for you to come in so I could get the rest of the scoop."

I lowered my voice. "Well, that corpse today might have had the last name Howard, and I'm just trying to figure out why he'd be here when he was in West Virginia until the day before Christmas."

Gina leaned forward on her elbow and dropped her voice to match mine. We probably looked like a couple of teenage gossip girls. "I heard he was a doppelgänger for Hoagie, except for the mole and the fact that the eyes were blue instead of deep brown."

"Yes, but why is what I want to know. And if he was already dead and embalmed, why was he here and how did he get here?"

"I don't know, but I look forward to what you come up with."

"Yeah, me too, though I don't know what that might be. Can you ask your mom to see how Hoagie is related to us? I just want to see if there's a branch of the tree I don't know about."

When I got back to the house, Max was there, puttering around the kitchen. I had a ton of room now, so I got out of his way while he made us a late dinner from all the leftovers my mom had sent us home with.

"What's up?" he asked, wiping his hands on his apron. It told me to "Kiss the Cook," so I did before I moved my laptop to the living room and rebooted.

"I have a line on the missing corpse, but I don't know what it means."

"That's some quick work."

"It was awkward work, and I really hope it pays off. Now shoo while I look up a few things, and then I promise to put it all aside while we eat dinner."

He laughed as he went back to the counter, where he had various containers laid out, and started assembling plates.

"No cranberry sauce," I called out.

"Yes, I'm aware of that, even if your mom hasn't gotten the clue yet."

Smiling, I pulled open my browser and typed in the parameters I had—Jerry Howard, West Virginia, death.

I had to refine it because there were quite a few Jerry Howards and many deaths over the course of the years. I wished I had asked the owner of the funeral home where he'd died or when, but I wasn't going to call him back. Instead, I pulled up newspaper articles and obituaries.

And found him.

I crowed as I watched his picture load on my monumentally slow laptop. I had him, and in life he looked even more like Hoagie. The resemblance really was uncanny. But why?

Reading over the obituary gave me nothing, but I still felt like I'd done some solid work.

I let Max know I'd be right back and then ran down three flights of stairs to give my dad the info and then called Burton with my dad standing over poor Jerry.

"It sure would be nice if the dead could speak, wouldn't it, Dad?" I asked as I waited for Burton to pick up.

"Not if their jaws are wired shut. I wouldn't be able to understand anything they'd say." He leaned back against the edge of the metal table used for preparing corpses in the basement.

I snorted in laughter after checking that he had actually made a joke. Maybe Max volunteering to help out had finally put the old man in a better mood.

"What, Tallie? I'm in the middle of things." Burton sounded less jovial, but that was okay.

"The corpse is Jerry Howard, recently deceased in West Virginia, and someone stole him from the funeral home down there, then transported him up here. He didn't have a dent in his head when he died. That was after."

Dead silence on the other end from Burton, though I could hear background noise that told me he was at the police station.

"Dare I ask how you got that info?" he finally said.

"You certainly may." And I was very proud to share, because it was all very aboveboard. "I called the funeral directors association and found out that an APB had been put out for a missing corpse. Called the completely incompetent mortician who did work on him and then lost him and verified his identity via the internet. It's creepy how much he looks like Hoagie. How do you think someone found him and brought him here?"

"And you seriously won't consider being a part of the force?" Burton asked.

I was taken aback for a second because he actually sounded serious for the first time ever. Normally, that was said with a load of derision behind it, but this time it almost sounded wishful.

"No, Burton, I'm better off where I am. I finally know what I want to be when I grow up, and it's not with you as a boss."

That got him to snort. "Yeah, I think we'd both end up under your father's care if we actually had to work together on a daily basis, instead of only when people around here can't keep their murderous tendencies to themselves."

"Truth right there." I smiled, even though he couldn't see it.

"All right, can you shoot me everything you've found? Did he have any relatives that are still living?"

I was prepared for that and patted myself on the back for making notes. "His wife, whose name is Wanda, but the funeral director says she's missing and didn't pay for the services yet, so he's not going to worry about anything until he finds her."

Burton hummed across the line. "I wonder if she killed him and didn't want anyone to find out and so brought him up here to dump his body once she stole him."

"That's more your territory than mine. I'm still trying to figure out who out of everyone who disliked Ronda disliked her enough to actually kill her."

"I'm telling you, it's almost always the spouse, and Hoagie being gone is a serious mark in the column that says he did it."

"I'm not arguing, but it just feels wrong."

"Wrong or not, it would make sense. She wasn't nice to him and maybe he had an insurance policy on her. We need to find out who inherits." He'd said that last part as if to himself, but I knew a way I could get the information, so I let him sign off and immediately called my friend and cleaning partner, Letty.

Time to clean house, and for that I needed to have a meeting with my ladies. For tonight, I was done. The timer in the kitchen went off and the smells drifting into the living room were too good to pass up. Tomorrow was soon enough to get back to body tracking and murderer finding.

"What's our schedule like this week, Letty?" After leaving the info I'd found in Burton and my dad's care last night and eating enough leftovers to almost be embarrassed, I'd texted my crew and asked them to meet me at the Bean in the morning. I was on a run for breakfast there every morning and wasn't yet ready to cut my streak short.

I figured I'd check in to see if I remembered correctly that one of Hoagie's children had scheduled us to clean up after their after Christmas party. I hadn't been able to find my calendar and didn't want to be wrong.

I had thought that eventually I wouldn't have much to do with the cleaning business anymore. Tallie's Queens of Squeegeedom could take care of themselves. I didn't call us that anywhere but in my mind. In fact, the company, as little as it was, had become Graver's Cleaning Crew.

I now had four employees, with Letty as my right-hand woman. She was practically the runner of the show, but she didn't want the responsibility of the taxes and check writing part, so I kept that and she got to do what she excelled at, which was clean to her big heart's content. As well as handling the first interviews for hiring and placing the jobs with the right person.

Or at least that was how it was supposed to work when

my dad bought the café next door to the funeral home. I had run the café for a few months and had just watched over the cleaning crew. But then my mother decided that she really enjoyed working at that café my dad had bought, enough to boot me out. There were no hard feelings for the boot, because I had been just about to ask if someone else could take over because I missed cleaning.

There was something so satisfying about taking a dirty place and making sure it absolutely shone that I just hadn't gotten from serving people before and after funerals. I thought the café was a great idea, and I was glad I'd tried it, but I had been doing the right thing all along and just never realized it until I'd removed myself from the joys of a clean house.

The café/reception area that Mom now ran next to my father's funeral home had taken off, with most people deciding to have the service inside the funeral home, the goodbye in the tunnel that connected the home to the new business and then move to the reception area to have the life celebration.

Sometimes they even brought over the urn to have one final lunch with the loved ones if we had done a cremation. Some people were uncomfortable with that, but others loved it. And when it came to burying someone who had meant the world to you, it was totally at your discretion how that was carried out. This was the no-judgiest of no-judgment zones.

But I had liked cleaning so much more and was happy I was back at it and working part-time when my family needed me at the funeral home.

"We're in good shape," Letty said as we sat down to coffee and crullers paid for from the Graver's Cleaning Crew bank account.

We were still waiting for the other ladies to show up for our company meeting, so I thought I'd talk to her about the more sensitive stuff before anyone else got there.

"I have the girls booked up for this week and into next," she continued. "We have several spots through the rest of the month and could take on another weekly cleaning if we can find one, but other than that, we're running smooth like a vacuum cleaner on a wood floor."

Smiling at her phrasing, I checked that particular worry off my list of things to be concerned about. At first, I'd been reluctant to take on Letty's friends, who'd been envious of her good fortune and fantastic deal with me. But they'd convinced me that we could be a formidable team if we were all under one umbrella instead of all working independently. I'd taken the chance, mainly worried and up nights thinking that maybe there wouldn't be enough work, but for once, I'd been completely wrong, like wrong to the extreme of wrong.

And never happier to be wrong. I had ended up taking a cut of all the jobs when Letty yelled at me for not paying myself for my time in handling all the business aspects. My bank account grew every month and I earned every penny by also taking on the responsibility of following up with anyone who had not paid their bill on time.

"Okay, that's good." I wasn't sure if I should mention Hoagie. We used to buy our cleaning products from him, but now we only bought things at the hardware store if we ran out at the last minute and didn't have time to order from the commercial supply company. So she knew him, but might not be as invested in him as I had been.

"Did you hear about Hoagie?" she asked before I could decide if I was being ridiculous.

"Yeah, and I found his twin dead behind the hardware store."

"Wait, his actual twin? He always said he was an only."

"Not his actual twin." Although that sparked something in my brain, and I wrote it down just in case I might be able to look into that later. Maybe they'd been separated at birth. I really needed to ask my mom about how Hoagie was related to us, and see if he'd had brothers and sisters. "And I didn't actually find him. Nathan saw him from his staircase behind the hardware store."

"It's so sad. And he's still missing, then?"

"Nathan's really torn up about it," Jenna said as she walked up, flanked by Camilla and Annie. They each took seats. She sat next to Camilla, who sat next to Annie, who rounded out the table.

Letty patted Jenna's hand. "He was one of the nicest people ever, even if I wasn't overly fond of his wife. I can't believe she's dead. But she must have been good in some ways or Hoagie wouldn't have stayed, right? I'd like to think she had redeeming qualities that only he knew about." There was her big heart hard at work. And then she asked the question everyone seemed to have at the top of their mind. "Who would do something like this?"

"I have no idea, but I'd like to know," I said.

"Nathan would too. He's helpless over at the store without the owner." Jenna sat back in her chair with a frown on her face.

"That's so strange to me." I stirred my coffee, staring

out the front window to the newly falling snow. "With how long he's worked there, I would think Nathan would have access to everything."

"Nathan did too, but that bi—Ronda decided it would be bad business." And then Jenna started crying. "Sorry, it's just that Nathan is so stressed out and we're fighting." Wiping her eyes, she tried a weak smile. "It'll be okay eventually. I know it. And Hoagie told Nathan he would make sure he was taken care of if anything ever happened, so we should be fine."

"You know if you ever need anything, all you have to do is ask, Jenna." I patted her hand this time, and she smiled a real smile through those tears.

"I so appreciate that, Tallie. I can't tell you how much that means to me. Right now we're okay because there's a bookkeeper who releases the paycheck into Nathan's account, without input from Hoagie. Thankfully, Nathan is on salary. And hopefully, soon Hoagie will be found and everything will be okay."

"In the meantime, don't forget to let me know if you need something."

"If something comes to me, I'll let you know. I just want the person who killed Ronda found and then find Hoagie himself."

I was working on that, but I thought it better not to let everyone know. So we got down to work.

"Okay, so we have a new opportunity on the table that I wanted to run by all of you. How do we feel about cleaning up after fires?"

A lively discussion followed, and in the end, the consensus seemed to be that we could at least try it during these few weeks. I thanked them all and sent them on their way.

And then it was just me and Letty sitting in the Bean.

"Are you going to be looking into it?" Letty's voice shook a little across the table.

"I'm currently in negotiations with Uncle Sherman and Burton."

Letty's laughter was muffled behind her hand, but I still heard it loud and clear. We were talking about death, so it wasn't a big laugh, but more of the kind of laugh when you surprise someone into being baffled by your statement to the point that they can't help but laugh. Yeah, that kind. And I was getting it across a meal I'd just footed the bill for. I looked around to make sure Mama Shirley wasn't paying any attention.

"Hey, at least there hasn't been any yelling yet, and if I can help in any way, I'd like to. After five suspicious deaths in town and being involved in solving each of them, I think Burton might actually value my opinion."

"There is that," Letty said. "So you'll be getting involved?"

"I'm going to try to use the tip line this time."

Another snicker from her. Traitor.

"I'm going to go now," Letty said, rising from her chair and taking her clean plate with her. "Go talk to Burton, or at least call him." She hummed to herself for a moment. "You know, I'm doing Chrissy Jessup's house this afternoon, if you want to make sure that we're all working to the level you think we should be."

My brain shot through the list of people I knew because that name was familiar. In a split-second, I came up with Chrissy Jessup, who had once been Chrissy Hogart, the daughter of the missing man known to those who had loved him as Hoagie. The man of the hour we were all looking for and someone dead had been impersonating.

Chrissy Jessup, who everyone had thought would marry Nathan and keep the store in the family.

How was that for fate?

Chapter Twelve

"Where is my vacuum? I have to have my vacuum and my squeegee, and that little caddy thing I had made for all the girls. Oh, and I can't forget to take my rags and that bottle of spritzer that I like to use on the mirrors." I ran around the apartment looking for all the things I usually kept in the back of the car. I'd taken them out for the holidays and had not planned on putting them back until after the first of the year.

I'd taken the week off between Christmas and New Year to spend with Max at Letty's insistence and so thought I'd have time to reload my car, but now I needed it pronto and didn't know where everything was.

Max put his hand on my shoulder. "It's all in here." He directed me to the small closet I'd used as a pantry since I'd moved in. Because we now had a real, honest-to-goodness pantry, Max must have put my supplies in the closet to keep them all together. Smart man.

I was happy to find all my cleaning equipment nicely and cleanly stacked in the small space. I started dragging out stuff and putting it on the floor behind me. I heard rustling and saw that Max had grabbed a dolly from next to the fridge and was loading it up with my things.

"You are just the sweetest," I told him, leaning over to kiss him on the cheek.

"All part of the service, ma'am," he responded in a horrible Spaghetti Western accent.

I nudged him with my shoulder and kissed him again. "You don't mind that I'm heading out to clean when I could be here, helping you, instead of snooping where I'm wanted but maybe shouldn't be anyway?"

"Let's just leave it at you're going to help Letty with a big job and keep everyone else in the dark altogether. Maybe that way Burton's ears won't be burning because we're talking about him, and he won't show up right where you are right at the wrong time, like he has before."

He was right. Burton might have said I could ask around about the corpse, but as for going to the deceased's kids, we hadn't talked about that.

Max's comment earned him a smile as I traipsed out the door and then hoofed it down the stairs with him following behind me. I carried some of the stuff and he had the rest on the dolly. The funeral home had an elevator, but it only went from the first floor to the basement, where the bodies were prepared for burial. Which did not help me at the moment.

Max and I shuffled out the back door to my waiting car. The hearses were back there too, but unlike the norm lately, no one had parked me in. Finally! Maybe me leaving sticky notes on every car's windshield with the words DO NOT PARK TALLIE IN OR I WILL FIND YOU AND PUT YOU IN THE BASEMENT had finally worked.

I opened the trunk of my old, beloved Lexus from days gone by and arranged all my cleaning paraphernalia in the back. When I turned around to say goodbye to Max, he grabbed me up in a big hug.

"Be careful out there, and don't forget to avoid trouble like you avoid bleu cheese dressing."

I laughed, gave him one last squeeze and then climbed into my car. I wasn't sure what I'd find at the Jessup house, or what information I could glean without seeming to even be interested beyond that of a concerned neighbor. But no one was going to stop me from at least trying.

In the end, I decided to play the so-sorry-for-the-death, let-us-know-if-we-can-help-with-anything-with-the-funeral bit. It had worked wonders before. I wasn't above using it again.

Pulling up at the Jessup house, I parked behind Letty and took a deep breath before opening the trunk of my car. I could do this. I could go in and talk to a woman who was my cousin to find out what she knew about her mother's death and enemies without losing it. I'd done it before and I would do it again. Hopefully not, but so far, my life away from Waldo had been a roller coaster of things. I'd survive this too, even if it was behind the mask of a dust wand and a vacuum cleaner.

I was good at what I did, be that working at the funeral

home, being a partner to Max, or cleaning houses. But Letty had always been better at cleaning than me and I wanted to talk to Chrissy to see what she had to say.

I shouldn't have worried. Letty met me at the back door with a smile and a quick hug.

"You know I love you and think that you do amazing things. But how about we leave the cleaning to me today and you work on wiping down the counters and keeping Chrissy company?"

"Are you saying I don't know what I'm doing?" I asked. "Because I do know what I'm doing, I'll have you know."

"Knock it off. We all know you're an awesome maid." She swatted me on the arm. "I've learned tons from you. It's only after having worked for you that I was able to up my game. Don't be an idiot. I'm just saying that if you stay near them without having to turn on the vacuum, it will be easier for you to talk with them." She pushed me farther into the house, through the mudroom, into a laundry room filled with the latest in technology. "The kitchen seems to be where they stay most of the time."

"Oh." I got momentarily distracted by the chrome stacked washer and dryer. I should have thought about that set before we bought the one in our new place.

"Yeah, don't even start with me. You know I love that you came back to cleaning with us again, and I gladly stepped aside without a single hesitation. But I know you're not actually here to clean, so I was trying to make it easier on you."

"Yeah, I wasn't picking up what you were throwing down there."

"Guilt?" She smiled at me.

"Some. I just don't want you to feel like I'm using

you, or be uncomfortable when you know I'm going to be asking questions that Chrissy might not want to answer."

She groaned and hit me again.

This one actually hurt. "Ow."

"That's for being an idiot. Now, let's go clean before the family comes out and starts trying to help us with things. Sometimes the kids like to carry around my caddy. I had to get those Mr. Yuk stickers to make sure they weren't messing with the chemicals because their parents don't always watch them."

Ah yes, I remembered that from when I used to clean this house. The youngest had run off with a bottle of bleach and made my heart stop. I didn't have kids and wasn't sure I ever would. I, of course, would not be telling my mom that; it was my secret, and not one I wanted her weighing in on, loudly and vehemently.

But even I knew you should watch kids around chemicals. When I was young, one lady down the street had mixed bleach and ammonia in her toilet and Uncle Sherman had to come out to air out the house because it was toxic. I'd learned my lesson that day and hadn't unlearned it since.

But those stickers made me think of Hoagie and Ronda, and I buckled down to get through some tough questions.

Letty and I headed farther into the house, loaded down with our caddies and our supplies. I had no plan whatsoever about what I'd talk about, or how I'd even start a conversation regarding this woman's dead mother and missing father, but I trusted my gut that something would come to me. If all else failed, I could fall back on the funeral excuse, though I was more and more reluctant to use it.

The first person we saw upon entering the spacious, blue-and-white kitchen was Todd Jessup, Chrissy's husband, standing over near a wine rack. He was just shy of six feet tall and had moved here from Montana years ago after meeting Chrissy during a rodeo or something.

Hoagie had made all his kids work during a gap year after high school. He'd said it built character. Though I had heard that he wasn't happy when Chrissy decided to actually leave the state; no one else had. But she'd snuck away one night on a bus, and no matter how much her dad had begged her, she'd stayed in Montana for six months, then come home married to Todd. And left Nathan hanging.

According to the grapevine, it was a happy marriage and their kids were good ones. And she was a talker, which hopefully would make my mission an easier one. Hopefully, though life seldom worked that way for me.

Looking farther into the kitchen, I spotted Chrissy.

"Tallie!" Chrissy sat at the kitchen table with some supermarket rag from the magazine stand. She loved gossip and had tried to take the title of "Gossip Hub" from Mama Shirley a few times but had never quite succeeded. Mama Shirley probably wouldn't give up that title even when she was dead.

"Hey, Chrissy. Just thought I'd come by with my crew to see how you're doing." I didn't use my dirge voice because she seemed happy enough. I didn't want her to start crying, but I also didn't want to answer her back as brightly as she had said my name.

"Oh." She closed the magazine. "Right."

That was an odd response, but I let it pass to see what more she would say.

"Mom's dead. Dad's gone. I'm sure you know."

"Yeah. I'm sorry about that. Ronda will be remembered fondly." I wasn't sure what to say about Hoagie, so I left it alone for the moment. Unfortunately, there was a distinct possibility that someone had taken him and left that body, hoping it would burn and no one would question it.

I got back on topic before I trailed too far away from my mission. "If there's anything I can do or if you need help, just say something. We're family, after all."

She snorted, and I very firmly reminded myself that everyone grieved and processed death differently. Just because she wasn't crying didn't mean she hadn't or that she wouldn't in the future when it hit her what had really happened.

"Your dad had everything set up at Graver's, so you won't have to worry about that." I stayed standing while she sat at the table because she hadn't invited me to take a seat yet. I didn't want to assume she had any desire to talk to me at all, so standing at least gave the illusion that I could walk away and start cleaning at any moment. Not that I would, but the illusion could be everything in the right circumstances.

"Well, that's something at least that we won't have to pay for, because no one but that coattail rider at the hardware store is getting a dime."

Now I did sit down, no matter what she wanted or didn't want. As far as I knew, Hoagie didn't have a ton of money, but he had valuable property and many contacts. That hardware store had paid for schooling, and vacations, and all the necessities for years. It had to be worth a pretty penny. And none of them were getting anything except the one person who wasn't related to Hoagie?

"Nothing for no one?" I asked, unable to resist trying to keep this conversation going.

"Correct, no one and nothing. Only Nathan is getting anything, and that anything is full control of the entire store and all assets. Because no one ever wanted to work at the family store, Dad decided to make sure no one ever could unless we worked under Nathan the Magnificent."

Wow, animosity, thy name was Chrissy! She was seething to the point that Todd stopped polishing the wine bottles in his cabinet by the fridge and came over to pat his wife's back. But why was she assuming that the store would go to Nathan right now, when Hoagie was still possibly alive?

"Now, honey, we talked about this. No one else wanted to run the store anyway and it's been a staple for years. Plus, we do fine without your father's money. Don't we?"

The grudging nod was not very reassuring, nor was the rolling of the eyes outside of Todd's vision, but I didn't say anything. Did she regret not marrying Nathan now that he was the only one to inherit?

I was sincerely hoping Todd would go back to polishing bottles in another room so I could drill Chrissy.

And then he did, moving with his towel to the next room and what I assumed was another rack of wine bottles.

I wasted no time scooting my chair closer. Chrissy liked to talk, and I was going to let her talk once I got the conversation rolling in the right direction. How to do that without coming off as awkward?

"This must be so hard after also losing Ronda," I said, reaching out to pat her hand.

She yanked it back and put it under the table. "We didn't

lose her. She was killed with a can from my dad's store. You found her, Tallie. Don't try to be coy. Everyone knows you're always trying to figure out things before the police do."

My cover was blown. Not that I'd really had one to begin with, because I wasn't cleaning anything and most people did know that over the last couple of years I was the one who handed Burton the perpetrator. Not that he had ever really thanked me for my services to the community until recently.

"I wasn't trying to be coy. I really am sorry. She was good people." I choked on that last part but would have said it about the devil's best friend if I had to.

"Yes, well, she at least I could count on to always be her nasty self. It's Dad that has a lot to answer for. He often was nice to anyone who wasn't living in his house. At home, he was a whole different kind of man."

Part of me shrank back at that. He might have been nasty sometimes, because everyone must have bad days. But he was just cranky, not actually a jerk. I didn't want to hear my memories of Hoagie tarnished. I did have good memories, and they were keeping me looking for him and looking into the man who could have been related to him. How else could the corpse look so much like Hoagie? And I didn't want him to be anything other than what he presented at the hardware store, with his sage advice, his big voice and his mile-wide smile.

She sneered from her hand-carved wooden kitchen chair and slapped a hand on the oak table. "See, no one wants to hear about that. Everyone only knows the Hoagie from the store, but I knew a different one, and no one ever believed me. Do you know what it's like to live with one outwardly horrible mother and a father who is only horrible once the front door is closed?" She sank back in her chair with her arms crossed and an expression of pure mutiny on her face.

I flinched, even though I'd heard worse things before.

Grieving people often chose one of two ways to express that grief. They either only talked about the good things, to make the deceased into an angel the earth had been blessed with, and we were so very lucky to have this inhumanly kind and wonderful person for any amount of time. Or they went the other way, and talked about how the person was so flawed that the world was better without them, and could we just put them in the ground now so it could be over? Of course there were people in between; rarely was anything so polarized all the time, but the ones who chose a side to sit on rarely moved off it.

"I'll listen." There, I'd said it, and now I was going to have to deal with whatever came out of her mouth. Whatever her brain had chosen to focus on while she dealt with her father taking off and her mother dead.

"He rarely let us go anywhere that wasn't the hardware store. He had so many rules, they had to write them out and post them next to the refrigerator. Don't be out past ten. Don't talk to strangers. Don't talk to people who think you're someone you're not. Don't give away our family connections. Don't ride your bike past the town limits. Don't ride in a car that doesn't belong to an immediate family member. The list went on."

Interesting. I hadn't realized that was how they'd been raised. "He seems almost paranoid."

"Ha! He was beyond paranoid, straight into superneurotic-to-the-nines paranoid. He about had a heart attack when I took off for Montana, but I'd never seen anything outside of our town. I wasn't even allowed to go to the mall to buy clothes without my mother or him hovering over me like someone was going to snatch me away at any minute. I know there were kids who got kidnapped all those years ago that were all over the television, like Adam Walsh and Elizabeth Smart, but my mom and dad took the Amber alert thing to the extremes. They'd go crazy if we were one minute late home from a dance, and those were only at school. With four of us, they somehow kept track of every single one. I'm so thankful we didn't have these phones that we do now when we were younger because I guarantee you, he would have had some kind of command center where he would know when we were going to the bathroom and whether or not we'd washed our hands."

I sat back, not sure how to take this all in. Obviously, it was not a horrible thing; there was nothing illegal or disgusting about wanting to make sure your kids were safe. Though of course I knew for a fact I would have gone bonkers if my parents had been that strict, but it wasn't against the law. And she still lived in town, so there must have been something she liked here.

"You came back from Montana with Todd, though. You could have stayed out there when you were already out."

She snorted and slapped her hand on the top of the magazine. Todd turned, but stayed where he was. I hoped he remained that way. "That's because my parents refused to come to us, and Todd wanted to be near family because he doesn't have any. If it had been only my choice, I would have lived on the other side of the world."

But that was over fifteen years ago, and Ronda had to have been a little lacking in those familial warm and fuzzies at least enough for Todd to even consider moving.

I didn't ask her the question that burned on my tongue—
the one about why she hadn't moved then because she
could have moved any time after that—because we were
getting off topic and I needed to get the story from her before Letty in all her efficiency was done cleaning the
house.

"So, do you have any idea who would have wanted
Ronda dead and Hoagie gone?"

"You want to know what I think? I think you should
look at Nathan. Mom was fighting Dad tooth and nail
about giving everything to Nathan but hadn't made any
progress as of yet. Maybe Nathan wanted to hasten things
along a little bit. Maybe he decided Dad had lived past
his shelf date, and Mom never would have given it up
without being forced to by Dad. So he killed Mom and
then went after Dad. I'd say he got the best of both worlds
with Mom and Dad gone. Look at that for a bit and see if
it doesn't make sense."

Chapter Thirteen

Yikes. I wasn't sure what to say to that. I knew Nathan a little and I didn't see him as ever thinking Hoagie had outlived his usefulness, especially with how nervous he was about not being able to run the store without him. And I certainly couldn't understand how he would think Hoagie should now go to the great drill press in the sky. However, I didn't want to contradict her and make her angry. Then she'd stop talking to me.

"Nathan? You think he might be the one?" And why would Hoagie have outright told his kids that they were getting nothing? And when had he done it? Timing could be everything.

"I wouldn't be surprised, that's all I'm saying. Nathan has been insinuating himself into Dad's good graces for years. We were even supposed to get married until I ran away to escape it. He's always wanted to take over the store. And we'll see about that. My oldest brother, Carl, is already talking to a lawyer because we should contest the will. There was an offer from a big corporation to buy out the hardware store that he brought to Dad and he refused. Well, now that he's gone, I think we should sell and all get a part of what kept us here, chained in one spot."

Todd came back in on that last sentence and shot Chrissy a narrow-eyed glare. She harrumphed and crossed her arms tighter over her chest, then turned her face away from him.

This was big talk when we didn't know for certain that Hoagie was anything more than missing, not dead. But maybe every time she'd said "gone" she meant dead. If Burton hadn't told her it was a twin corpse, maybe I shouldn't either.

Trouble in paradise here? Differing thoughts on what should happen and when it should happen? They seemed like a nice couple, but sometimes those were the ones you had to worry about the most.

Fortunately, Letty peeked around the corner into the kitchen and gave me a nod. The cleaning was done and we could now leave. I hadn't lifted a finger physically, but my brain was working overtime with the information I'd found out. Part of me wanted to share it with Burton and the other part wanted to make sure I had all the information I could get before saying anything.

I did, however, feel it might be a good thing to check what story he was letting people believe before I went anywhere else.

I said my goodbyes and offered to help in any way I could again, with or without the funeral home, and then followed Letty outside.

We walked to our cars, hauling all of our things in silence. My brain was on overdrive and I didn't know where to start. Did I want to go after Nathan? But he'd been checking us out at the register when the fire alarm went off. And he'd seemed genuinely surprised when he saw the Hoagie look-alike. He'd seemed horrified to see him in the gravel outside the door.

And before that, he'd still been at the ball cage when Ronda had died. Or at least I thought so. Maybe? I couldn't remember. I'd picked up Ronda's purse and gone to give it to her, but I hadn't known where all the players were because I hadn't thought it was going to be important. I would have to ask around.

But first Burton, if I could get him to take my call. As much as I got involved, I still tried not to lie, at least not a lot, or at least not lies that could be easily found out. And Hoagie being officially dead was one of those times where it would be much better to be on the up and up. Was he letting people think Hoagie was dead to help the investigation along? Or was Chrissy assuming? Or had she killed him *and* her mom and was covering up her crimes?

Just because the corpse at the hardware store wasn't Hoagie didn't mean he was definitely still alive and running around.

I didn't want to sit in the jail again, rattling my plastic water bottle against the bars because they wouldn't give me a tin coffee cup. Burton would do it just for obstruction of justice if he got angry enough. He'd done it before without hesitation.

After putting her things in her trunk, Letty turned to me. "So, what did you find out?"

"I'm not really sure, to be honest. There's so much rolling around in this poor brain of mine that I don't know where to start. I have a ton of pieces, but I feel like they're from seventeen different puzzles instead of just one."

She put a hand up to stop me. "You'll get it right. I heard you grilling her, even if I didn't hear everything she said. Maybe you need to write it down in your trusty notebook and talk it over with Max. That seems to be the way you do things. Right? Todd kept giving looks over his shoulder to monitor the conversation. I really felt like he would have stepped in if Chrissy would have said anything he didn't want her to say."

"That's weird, because I felt the same way, and I've been cleaning their house for a while yet never felt that before. They'd always seemed like very happy and healthy people together. But today, I got this vibe that all is not what it seems."

She shook her head. "Do you think it's because of the murder?"

"I honestly don't know. I mean, I guess that's a possibility, but I feel like if I look back, it might have always been there, just not as strong as it was today, because we often talked about kids, or things going on around town, not murder."

Leaning back against her trunk, she eyed me. "So, what are you going to do now? I don't clean Nathan's house because I'm pretty sure Jenna does that for them, so I'm not in a position to help you get to him."

I laughed. "You don't have to be my pass into everywhere. And I hesitate to involve Jenna when she works for me and she and Nathan are fighting. I don't want to add to their troubles."

"Oh, I know you get in plenty of places all on your own. But this murder and second corpse is just baffling.

The other people who have died under mysterious circumstances have always seemed to be bad in their own right, but this one just feels different. And with Hoagie missing, there almost has to be more going on than a hidden secret that someone doesn't want to get out or a business deal gone wrong."

"Actually, I think you are incredibly right. And I'm with you on this one being something bigger. I guess I could go see if Nathan needs any help now that the store is closed for a bit for water damage. Jenna's working at the moment, and I could offer my help without it seeming too weird."

"It's a sound plan, or at least as sound as any of your plans tend to be."

I stuck my tongue out at her and she giggled.

"So mature, Tallie."

"I can't be all things adult."

"And I wouldn't have you any other way."

We left just as the front door opened. Todd stood in the doorway with his arms crossed and a stern look on his face, as if giving us warning that we had taken too long to get off his property.

Was it just a death in the family that was making him overly negative, or had he always been like that and I had just never noticed it? It was worth checking out, and I knew exactly who I was going to see after I'd talked to Nathan. Once I found him.

The hardware store was cordoned off with tape when I drove by on my way back home. A big, black banner ran across the front doors with the words "We Miss You" spelled out in hammers. Who had done that? And why were they assuming that Hoagie was dead? Or were they really missing Ronda? I had a hard time believing that last one, but stranger things had happened before.

I still had three other children belonging to Hoagie to talk with. Maybe they didn't all feel like Chrissy, or maybe she just thought they did because that was what she wanted . . .

She had been the black sheep in her family for years. It could be that she wanted them all to feel like she did, but they didn't. It bore thinking on to come up with a way to talk to the others without seeming like I was talking to them. But Chrissy might have warned them that I was looking into things and therefore they wouldn't talk to me at all.

I needed to put Max on doing some background digging.

I did want to find out if Nathan really was the only inheritor of the hardware store, though. That felt like it would be significant if it was true. And when had Hoagie's children been told?

But no one answered after I walked up the two flights of metal stairs to knock on Nathan's door. He would have to wait. I texted Jenna to see where she was, and if she knew where her husband was. When an answer didn't come back right away I figured I'd hear from her soon enough.

Which led me to the other side of Main Street, where I could get my caffeine fix, my sugar fix, and my gossip fix, all at the same time. Mama Shirley would give me that last one while my best friend, Gina Laudermilch, could give me the other two in spades.

The Bean There, Done That sat on Main Street in all its glory. It had been the scene of a crime a little while back, but that smudge on its reputation was nothing compared to the way it shone in the early afternoon sunlight. I was fully aware this would be my second visit in one day, but who else was counting? Not Gina, because my money spent like everyone else's and she didn't even give me a discount.

People came in and out of the front door to the point that Gina had removed the bells that jangled above it. It was too distracting to have them going off all the time, in her opinion.

So nothing jangled when I pulled the door, but the din of conversation probably would have drowned everything out anyway. The place was stacked with people at the lunch counter, in chairs at the tables. And one topic of conversation dominated the whole place.

The Hogarts.

I caught bits and pieces of people who were sad and others that were laughing at the things the man had done over the years. From the time he'd worn a top hat every day throughout the year until he'd started going bald in a fringe like a friar, to the time he'd run a huge train around the whole store to make the kids laugh at Christmas. No one said a word about Ronda, just Hoagie and the way he'd given to the community, and some speculation about where he might be, though most were talking as if he were indeed dead.

Lester Walkins had a story about the way he'd refused to prosecute a shoplifter and had instead taught him to shelve and stage the store to the point where he'd become a professional and now set up box stores across the country to make them shine. Lester was on the side who thought Hoagie was on his way to eternity.

Fran Keller, who thought Hoagie was just hiding out

somewhere, told a story about the time Hoagie decided that Halloween should be celebrated on the day it actually was set on the calendar, instead of the Thursday before, like the borough had set aside. It was a huge bone of contention within the community. To this day, unless October 31 fell on a Thursday, kids in our area never got to actually trick-or-treat on Halloween. The borough said it was for safety reasons, with the traffic on Friday or Saturday nights. Most of us didn't understand and thought it was ridiculous yet left it alone to fight other, bigger battles with the borough.

But one year Hoagie decided to take Halloween back and handed out candy, had a parade in the store, and dressed up as Santa Claus on the day itself. The town had come after him, and he'd mock-battled with the officer in charge of the arrest all those years ago.

I think it was Burton at that point, too. Poor guy never seemed to get a break.

We kids had loved having two Halloweens, and from then on, we could always dress up on the actual holiday and go into the store for candy. We hadn't had a parade in years, and Hoagie hadn't dressed up himself again, but it had been a fun thing for those who wanted it to be the holiday itself.

He'd done a lot for the community, and the community would be behind him, to support him in the death of his wife no matter how many people hadn't liked her. But where was he? Unless he'd killed her. And I'd bet dollars to the doughnuts I was eyeing in the bakery case that some would still be behind him even if he'd done the deed.

A few people whispered to one another, including Jenna and her friends. She'd never texted me back about talking with Nathan, and I might need to corner her. I had thought she still had another house to clean, but I could have been wrong without my calendar. I'd check that too, just as soon as I got the scoop on everything else.

I wished those whispered words were the conversations I could hear, but aside from plunking myself down right outside their sphere and figuring out how to get an invisibility cape in the process, it wasn't going to happen. However, there was always Mama Shirley, who would know what everyone was saying regardless.

Gina gave me a sad smile when I came up to the counter. She'd already made me a steaming cup of cookies and cream coffee mixed with hot chocolate. I had been hesitant to try it when she'd first put it on the menu, preferring my whoopee pie latte, but then I'd fallen in love with it. I didn't mean to cheat on my favorite coffee, but this one was pretty stellar all on its own.

"So, have you found out anything more about the dead guy?" she said as I bellied up to the counter.

"I haven't. I think I figured out who he was, though, but I don't understand why he would have been here in the first place. He was already dead and embalmed in West Virginia. Someone moved him here. But who?"

One of her eyebrows shot up. "That's a lot of work in very little time."

"Not really."

"Let's not play games. What are you going to do about it? Burton was already in here, talking with Mama Shirley. I don't know what about, because she won't tell me, but they looked pretty serious."

He had invited me to help. He'd better not be going around my back to cut off my primo, number one source of information . . .

"Of course she told him to mind his own business and she'd mind hers, and if he'd figure it out on his own, you wouldn't have to be involved anyway."

I snickered, because that was a good one. I'd have to tell her that when I saw her. It was something I'd been saying for a while. It's not like I wanted to get involved with all these murders. In fact, I'd rather they stop altogether, but that didn't appear to be happening, so we needed to figure them out as soon as possible to make sure the killers were behind bars. Or at least off the streets, so the town would be safer. And if that meant I solved things to make my town a safe place, so be it.

"Where is Mama Shirley?" I asked, taking a sip of pure heaven with a shot of caffeine.

"She's down at Carl's to see if there's anything she can do to help. She and his wife play bingo together, and that's like a sisterhood. Not quite the Bingo Queens, but it's close."

Dang it! I wished I could be in that sisterhood, but I didn't play a lot of bingo. And I refused to get a Bingo Queen tote made to carry around my own set of troll dolls.

I'd tried once to fit in with the bingo crowd, and my grandmother on my father's side, who was a die-hard, had threatened not to let me ride home in her car after I won, because only those who had devoted their lives to it should win, according to the old guard. And anyone who was not a die-hard was not anymore welcome to play than the crowd had welcomed those non die-hards on Christmas Eve.

"Well, when you see her, tell her I have a few questions. Unless you know how Hoagie is related to us. I guess I could ask my mother, but I'm almost afraid to go over there. I'm trying my hardest to stay away from my grandmother for a little while longer."

"Hmmm." Gina wiped the clean counter as she thought. "He's someone's uncle, though I can't remember who. Chrissy, Carl, Caitlin and Calvin are all cousins of yours, but then again, around here we seem to call anyone close to us who's related in any way a cousin. I'll ask and get back to you. But it might be better for you to just go to the source."

"My grandmother, remember?"

"She's not so bad."

"Yeah, but that's only because you're new to the family. She'll want to keep you happy until that second ring is on your finger."

Gina glanced down at her left hand and smiled. "After that, I'll handle her."

"I'll look forward to that with much anticipation. In the meantime, did you know that the hardware store is going to be left to Nathan, and the kids pretty much get nothing? Chrissy told me when Letty and I were over there a few hours ago to clean."

"Well, then, it can't be one of the kids who murdered her."

I tapped a finger on the counter. "That doesn't process. Why not? They could have been angry about how things were going and killed her to get the store."

"But you just said they aren't getting anything, and if Chrissy knows that, I'm sure she's spread it to anyone who would listen. They would have waited until the will was changed. Killing her now took away all their options. Unless they thought they could coerce Hoagie into changing things without Ronda here. Although I don't get why he would have gone into hiding then."

That was something to think about. "I see your point, but I'll up you one more that if they didn't wait, the will was never going to be changed back."

"Which would mean they weren't getting anything at all, no matter what," Gina finished for me.

I stuck my chin on my upturned palm and considered. "Do you think it's weird that we talk about murder and inheritance in the same way we'd talk about what aroma of coffee is best?"

Her smile was small, but turned into a chuckle. "Not at all. In fact, I think it's one of our best qualities."

Mama came busting through the back at her words. "You have many good qualities, but the best is your ability to keep your thoughts to yourself when they shouldn't be given to anyone else."

That sounded a little like a smackdown. I flinched with my coffee in my hand, almost splashing it on myself.

Gina looked sheepish too.

"Both of you, in the back." Mama surveyed the coffee shop her daughter owned, nodded as if what she saw pleased her, and then turned around. She went into the back room, knowing we would follow her, counting on it because we knew if we didn't, she'd come back out and drag us by the arms if she had to.

I scrambled off my seat and came around the corner, pulling Gina behind me when she hesitated. "You know what's expected," I whispered.

"And what if I want to pretend that I'm an actual adult and don't need to listen to my mother's every command?" she said back, but I noted she whispered also.

"Problem in mommyland?"

"She won't leave the whole getting-married-to-your-brother thing alone. She wants it soon. Heck, she wants it last month. But I want time to plan the wedding I've dreamed of, and she's not listening. I'm tired of it."

"I know you're saying things even if I can't hear them," Mama said from behind the closed door to the back.

I patted Gina's arm. "We'll talk later. For now, let's just see what she has to say, then go from there."

Gina's lips pressed firmly together, but she didn't utter another word. Good enough.

Mama Shirley was smiling at us very pleasantly when we came through the door to join her in the break room. "Girls, I'm not going to scold you. You're making this old woman feel like I'm a meanie."

"Of course that's not our intention," I said before Gina could chime in. "You just looked mad."

"But it's not at you, it's at that dolt, Burton, who keeps telling me what I can and can't do. He has to have learned over the past sixty years that that doesn't work with me. So now we're going to go top secret."

That I could be on board with. Even Gina smiled.

"What did you find out?" she asked her mom.

"It's what I didn't find out that's more interesting."

Chapter Fourteen

"I can't find Hoagie on your family tree." Mama Shirley announced this as if it should have been intoned instead of said.

It took me a moment to follow what she was saying. "Did you look in the right place?"

She shot an eyebrow up at me that matched the one from Gina earlier. "Of course I did. And he's not there."

"Wait, do you have an actual tree for everyone in town? Like on a wall in a gallery, the way Sirius Black did?"

Gina laughed. "She is not going to know what you mean by that, Tallie, because she only watches her daytime soaps. We don't have actual trees on walls, but Mama does have a book where everyone's name and place is kept, and if Mama says he's not there, he's not there."

"But we are related, right?" I asked a second, obvious question and got a frown in return.

"I don't know," Mama said. "I talked to several of your relatives, and they all agree that he's related to them but can't remember how."

"Did you ask Burton?"

"That's the strange part. He said it was through your Aunt Bertha, but I know where that page is and he's not there. And Hoagie's never been like a relation that was born on the wrong side of the blanket, or someone who married in. I distinctly remember that he and his family were a solid branch of the tree going back decades, but the more I think about it, the more I realize I don't know where that started or where it came from. When I pressed Burton, he got pissy and then pretended to take a call to get me out of his office. The darn phone didn't even ring, but he picked it up and started talking as if it had."

"Rude," I said, baffled that Burton would do that to his favorite cousin. They might have had their differences over the years, but he always came in for coffee and to talk with Mama, knowing that nine times out of ten she'd have more info than he could legitimately pay for from an informant.

"Did he hang up when you walked out?" Gina asked.

"I don't know because I was in a huff, but I went in there to see which child he had contacted to make the funeral arrangements, and who he thought might come so we could make sure the whole family was taken care of, so I decided to do some looking on my own. But I cannot for the life of me find out who Hoagie is actually related to."

"That is bizarre." My mind was in high gear as I took a seat on the couch. That only lasted for a second, though, as I popped back up fast enough to have my knees cracking. "I feel like Burton's hiding something. I thought he was being truthful with me and really wanted my help, but now I'm not so sure. And why is there so much focus on Hoagie and not on finding Ronda's killer? It's like she's being left in the dust." Could he be playing me? Letting me think I was helping and then running me in circles until he figured it out on his own?

"You're not the only one." Mama stood as ramrod straight as the small set of lockers Gina had installed for the employees she seemed never to be able to keep. "I talked with Gladys Newberry, second cousin once removed from your mother. And she wasn't able to remember either, and she's the genealogist in the family."

The plot thickened. "So, do you think Burton is trying to hide it, or do you think he feels dumb for not knowing?"

"I'm not sure, but I'll find out and get back to you. I want you girls to be careful, though. I have a bad feeling about this one. Please don't make my mother's intuition go off the scale."

With that, she left, hell-bent on her mission.

Gina and I turned to each other. "Thoughts?" I asked.

"I'm really not sure. I mean, Hoagie was always an uncle, but then, he seemed to be an uncle to everyone. Even I called him Uncle Hoagie until I was about twenty."

"I'm trying to think back over the years, but nothing strange is popping up for me," I said. "It's not always a perfect thing to do the family heritage, and I know he came to our family reunions for years, as long as they were in town. So I'm not sure what to think. He'll always be my uncle in my heart, but I guess it might be possible that the blood connection isn't really there."

"It's possible, but that just makes everything that much more bizarre."

"I'm thinking we should leave that to your mom and go off on the Nathan-and-other-siblings angle. Someone killed Ronda, and that's more important than finding Hoagie, unless they're one in the same. Should we divide and conquer?" I'd often asked Gina to help with these things because the one time I hadn't, she'd had a fit.

"Dividing and conquering might be in our best interest at this point. But you'd better keep me in the loop this time."

I rolled my eyes at her in plain view. "Of course I will. We're a team."

"But we haven't always been . . ."

Was she talking about the time I'd walked away to get married to that jerk Waldo and left all my friends behind, or the time I solved the murder of one of my former employers without her? I wasn't sure I was ready to ask, so I let it go.

"Look, I have dinner with the family tonight, and my uncle Sherman is going to be there again, along with my grandmother. Sherman tends to know what's going on around town, so I'll mine that info cave, and you keep at it with Mama Shirley and listen for gossip around the coffeehouse. Someone must know something about this guy. He's been here for years. It's just not possible that no one knows where he came from and who might have had it in for him." I realized I'd left out Ronda just like everyone else had been and felt bad. "We also need to figure out who killed his wife, though the longer he's gone, and with that body at the store, I wonder if it really was him that killed her. Do you think he found someone who looked like him and picked him up to throw us off the trail?" It seemed too weird to be a coincidence, so my mind was trying to slot it into a place that would make it make sense. It wasn't working, but at least I was trying.

"I have no idea. I guess that would make as much sense as anything, but how would he have known that there was someone who looked just like him in another state?"

"I have no idea. And that's a huge problem." I was at a loss as to where to even start.

"It is, but one I think we can handle if we put our heads together."

"You're right. We can do this. I'm going to go start looking around and talking to people, seeing what I can find, and then we'll reconvene."

Gina agreed and we went our separate ways after I grabbed my coffee and a doughnut to go.

Crossing the street to my home above the funeral home, I quietly walked up the back stairs to my third-floor apartment. My mother was doing something in the office and I didn't want to bother her. Of course, what that really meant was that I didn't want her bothering me, or asking me what I was doing, when I was going to get married instead of just living with Max, when I was going to start having babies or telling me to keep my nose out of this or my dad wouldn't be happy. All that could wait for dinner, later tonight. I'd been told to be at the house around eight o'clock. I was sure my grandmother would already be asleep by then, but my mother scoffed at me and demanded we show up.

I found Max up to his elbows in vegetables. Large knife in hand, he turned to me with his eyes crinkling. I was going to assume that meant he was smiling about the vegetables and not considering how he could kill me. I kissed him on the forehead, the one spot that probably didn't have any food debris on it, and went to go find Peanut.

The dog and my cat had become fast friends, and they were often found entwined on some piece of furniture. I didn't quite remember how I had lived without this big ball of fur. She was friendly and soft and generally well-behaved. Completely the opposite of Mr. Fleefers, who hissed at me when I went to pet him.

"You can just calm yourself down, you rascal. I have things to do, but I wanted to say hi before I got down to them." If the cat could have stuck out his tongue at me, it was a sure bet he would have. Instead, he circled on his perch on Peanut's back where she lay in the sun, then turned his back on me.

I petted Peanut anyway, ignoring the cat, and then went to the dining room table. It was wonderful to have more space up here. For a while now, I'd been living in what was essentially a studio apartment, complete with a Murphy bed that came down from the wall. But with Max taking up residence, we needed more space. Thank goodness we'd been able to expand, and all without killing each other. At least so far. I called a miracle on that.

Of course at that moment, I heard a loud yelp and a thump.

"You okay in there?" I yelled, not exactly wanting to go into the disaster zone to see what had happened.

"Yeah, yeah," he yelled back. "Just a little something I wasn't expecting."

"We have dinner this evening at my parents, again." And yes I had said that right. The leftovers in the fridge from Christmas were still good, but tonight was my grandmother's old school meat loaf, and I wasn't missing that for anything. I liked leftovers as much as the next person, but we were also celebrating some more tonight. We hadn't done much of that when I'd married Waldo, but then, there hadn't been much to celebrate because it was me running away from my family instead of bringing someone in who not only fit but made our family better. Waldo had certainly not done that.

"What time do you want to stop your master cheffing and get ready?" I knew I was going to have to shower and assumed he would too. We had two full bathrooms now, but the water pressure was better if you only ran one at a time.

"It'll only take a few minutes. You go ahead and do what you need to, and then give me a holler about thirty minutes before we have to go."

I took a quick shower and left my hair to air dry in case Max was ready to clean up. Instead, the whine of a food processor or a mixer or something mechanical started up, so I put my mind to my notes and organizing my thoughts. What on earth was he making? I didn't remember any big tools being used in the cookbook I'd gotten him for Christmas.

I let it go to concentrate on what I had and what I still needed to know about this latest mystery in town.

Burton agreed I was allowed in on this and appeared to actually want me on this case. That was different, but in a good way. I'd often been warned or cautioned, told and further cautioned, but this time felt different. Mama Shirley's warning that she didn't feel good about this one also gave me pause. On any other given day, she was knee deep in the mystery, but her mother's intuition wasn't to be ignored, or only ignored with caution.

So what was going on?

The facts were that Hoagie was missing and Ronda was dead. And we had a corpse with a dent in his head and a screwdriver in his back. But had he been put there after the fire alarm went off? And who had done it? I was still fighting naming Hoagie in all of this, but the more I heard about wills and inheritances, the more I wondered if I was just being naive.

Then what did this tell me? I tried writing circles on my paper and doodling, writing out my name and drawing little cars, but nothing was sparking. I glanced up at the clock on the stove. I didn't panic because we had time to spare, and I was going to take it to talk to Max about what I knew and what I'd like to know.

Hoagie had been a good guy and he deserved everything. Ronda not so much, but even she hadn't deserved being killed with a can of varnish to the head. I wondered if they'd bury her with her bingo bag full of good luck charms, the one she'd never been without.

That made me smile and also made me wonder if we had her in house just yet. Along with the corpse named Jerry.

Had Ronda's effects been returned to her kids? Which one? I could always go check in with Chrissy again, but I would rather not. I much preferred her sister Caitlin. It wouldn't take long to see if there was anything she needed. Burton would probably be grateful to me for getting involved by doing my job as an employee of the funeral home and providing the services we offered to those who knew us well . . .

I had time to search for more information. I told Max I was running out for a few and he just grunted. I was aware I was not being as truthful as I expected him to be with me, but I would own that if it came out later. Right now, I had a house call to make and a schedule to check downstairs.

After a quick change into black pants and a turquoise, short-sleeved, shell top covered by a black cardigan, I ran down the stairs to the second floor, where the computer with the schedule was kept. Logging on, I checked the master list my dad had for every person who had ever signed up for our services. After I opened the file for the Hogarts, I scanned the items and found that no one had yet talked with the family beyond letting Caitlin know that it might be a few days before the body was released to us.

Excellent. I left a note in the Comments section to say that I was taking the task of meeting with her in her home and seeing if she had an outfit picked out for her mother to be buried in.

Someone would see it, or they would apologize to her when they asked twice. Either way was fine with me.

I headed back down the street and walked the block to

Hoagie's house first to see if anyone might be there. I could have started at Caitlin's, but my instinct was that someone had to be at the house, and she lived next door to her parents, so I'd pass it on the way.

The hardware store did not have living quarters above it as so many of the buildings on Main Street did. Instead, Hoagie and his wife had bought the house four doors down and made it a home. I'd been over there for game nights when I was friends with their kids in high school. I played a mean round of rummy tile, if I did say so myself.

Eventually, we'd drifted apart, but I might need to call up some of those old connections if I couldn't get the info I was looking for. Like how Hoagie and his family were related to us, why no one seemed to be able to place him and who might have had it out for the man who had seemed to take immense enjoyment in selling nails, bolts, mailboxes and specially mixed paints. And why kill his wife? That was the most important question, and the one I seemed to have the least amount of information regarding.

Caitlin Rhodes answered the door in a black dress with swollen red eyes. Man, did I want to do this? It was one thing to interview and probe when the spouse was angry, or I thought they were the ones who might have done it. But this felt like stepping on a grieving daughter's toes when she'd already broken them by kicking a doorframe.

I stepped back and reassessed my motives in a split second. I wanted to find out who had done this to Ronda and where Hoagie was. I wanted to help, but I was going to have to tread lightly, and I was going to have to do it delicately and nicely, and without any hint that I thought anything was wrong.

With that, I took Caitlin's hands into my own, patted her fingers and told her how sorry I was for her loss. "I can come back later if you want me to. I don't want to catch you at a bad time."

"Oh, Tallie, I don't know that there's ever going to be a good time again. Come in, come in."

I held out the plate of snickerdoodles I'd thought to grab from the kitchen and the bouquet of flowers I'd stopped at Monty's flower shop for. The blooms were beautiful, a small spray of roses and daisies mixed together.

"They're lovely," she said as she opened the door wider and beckoned me in.

"I can come back if you'd rather wait."

"No, it's okay. Of course we knew Mom wasn't going to live forever, but the way she went out was horrible, and now such a senseless accident in the store my dad loved is just hard for me to process, you know?"

I didn't know because I was almost positive that the scene outside the hardware store had been anything but an accident. And it hadn't been Hoagie. Or was that what people still thought? I'd heard some people talking about his death at Gina's, but I would have thought Burton would have quelled those rumors due to the fact that the corpse hadn't been Hoagie. Was Burton allowing people to think Hoagie was dead when in fact it wasn't him and he knew it? Was that what Burton had told her? Had Burton made up a story to see if he could get people to talk? Had he told her he'd been hit like Ronda? Strangled? That he'd died from smoke inhalation? Why would he have let the rumor perpetuate when it obviously wasn't true?

I had forgotten to track him down to ask him when Mama Shirley had hit me with the Hoagie's-not-on-our-family-tree thing.

Regardless, I felt my blood boiling for a moment, then turned the burner down to simmer before I got too worked up. This could of course be the story she was telling herself to be able to get through the next few days. People often changed events to make them easier to manage if the truth was just too much to take in.

I could work around this. And it was something I'd have to put in the computer as soon as I got back to the funeral home. Dad needed to know she was not currently dealing with reality so he could work with it too in the best way he knew how.

"We are so sorry for your loss."

She led me to a floral couch done in primary colors. It was eye-popping and supercomfortable. If they had it in other colors, I might have considered it if we hadn't already bought all the furniture we needed. I wasn't buying anything again for a long time.

"Thank you so much. And thank you for the flowers. Dad used to send them to Mom for special occasions. Then again, he'd say every day was a special occasion." She sniffed and pulled out a handkerchief. I was not a fan of those things because they were always then stuffed back into a sleeve, a pocket or a purse after they'd been used, but who was I to judge?

"He is sorely missed." That was vague enough without playing into her wrong assumption that he'd died at the hardware store. "I remember working for him one summer and what a wonderful man he was." I'd worked for nearly everyone in town at some point, anything to get away from working at the funeral home. And look where I ended up anyway.

"He was a wonderful man. My dad. So kind, so giving, so generous with his time." She stared into the bouquet as if lost in time and space.

"You have your siblings to help you through this, right? And we're here."

She scoffed. "Yes, the others are already squabbling about what to do with the hardware store. One wants it sold, the other wants it rented out, one wants the contents donated to some organization for charity and then to transform the space into an art gallery. They're all ignoring the fact that Nathan already owns it outright. Dad had no intention of it going to any of us." She looked perfectly okay with that, which surprised me. Out of all of Hoagie's kids, she was the only one who was fine that she'd get nothing? I'd have to find out.

But holy schnikes. Well, Chrissy had been right and yet was wrong when we'd talked earlier. Not everyone had an issue with Nathan getting the store. I just nodded and filed that away, along with the information that she thought her dad was actually dead instead of some other poor guy who was transferred hundreds of miles to be propped against the store.

"Do you have any idea who would want your mother gone?" I waded in with the question that was haunting me, but in a gentle voice.

"I think you should talk to Chrissy about that." Her eyes hardened and she fisted her hand around the flowers.

"Chrissy? I talked to her, and she seemed to think I should talk to Nathan."

One derisive burst of laughter came out of her before she scowled fiercely. "Nathan would never have done anything to our parents. He loved them. More than my sister did, in fact. Of course she's going to point you to her old boyfriend. She's still angry that she's stuck with Todd."

"Really?"

"Absolutely. She wants the store but never put anything into it, and no matter how mean she told you our father was, it was nothing compared to the absolute lockdown he put on the rest of us when she went to Montana and wouldn't come back."

Well, this was more information than I had, so I ran with it. "She didn't seem to want the store and Todd made a point of telling her that they did fine without your father's money."

She snorted. "They do not. My father paid their mortgage almost every month because all Todd does is buy wine he never drinks so he can look like a more sophisticated person than he is. And my sister isn't much better."

"So you don't get along? I remember you all being friendly to one another. More than my siblings and I were."

Waving her hand in the air, she snorted again. "It was all a show, and one we were told to put on unless we wanted our backsides bruised. My dad had to keep up appearances and yet always wanted to stay under the radar."

"But he was always the one standing out front in our community."

"Ah, yes, the community. He embraced that and wanted

to appear to have no problems, but I wasn't kidding when I said we weren't allowed to go anywhere after Chrissy left. It was like he put a barbed wire fence around this town. No one got out. And no one could come in."

"Any idea why?"

She shrugged, and I wanted to scream. "I have no idea, but I will tell you that recently he was complaining because of some long-distance phone calls my mom was making. He burned a whole pile of letters while she sobbed her eyes out. Mom said we had an aunt somewhere in the south, and that was who she was calling, but Dad was against that and laid into her. No one else ever saw that side of him, but we did. I'd bet almost anything he had something to do with her death. I doubt he hit her with the varnish can, but he had his hand in other people's pockets."

"Hoagie?" I just couldn't take it in. After all these years, why would Hoagie want his wife dead? Unless it had to do with his disappearance.

"Yes, the wonderful and generous Hoagie. You know that's not even his real name? Who names their kid Hoagie anyway?" She sniffed and buried her face in her flowers. When she lifted her gaze, it was tear-drenched. "But no matter what, I still miss him and I can't figure out why." Sobbing, she doubled over.

I patted her back but couldn't think of anything else to say at the moment. Everything I thought I knew was being negated. But only by his two daughters. What did his two sons think of the whole thing?

When the tears finally ran out, I handed her a tissue from the box on the side table. She had that handkerchief, but this was too big a job for that small square of linen.

"Thank you. I'm not sure what came over me. I know it's all going to be okay. We'll get through this. We always do."

That was my cue to leave. I was pretty sure I had all the information I could possibly get out of her.

"Is there anything else we can be doing for you? Not just as a final resting place, but as neighbors and friends and relatives, Caitlin? My heart is with you during this difficult time. I don't want you to feel alone." That might have been laying it on a little thick, but I needed to get out of there and get together with Burton. What was he telling people? I really needed to know before I did anything more.

"You're a sweetheart, Tallie, but there's really nothing to do. Your father had been such a blessing in getting everything set up well in advance and he has it all in hand as soon as they release my dad and mom. The celebration of life will be lovely and the flowers are already all picked out from Monty's. Thank you, though. It means a lot to me that you came out."

"It's not a problem."

"You come from a good family."

The doorbell rang, and she smiled gently.

"And that must be your father. He'd called just a few minutes before you came in to see if we could meet. I'm sure he'll be happy to see you stopped by."

"Uh, of course." He hadn't put any notes in the computer, blast him!

And now I was stuck, because I couldn't run out the back door without him knowing I had been there. Caitlin wouldn't understand if I told her to keep it a secret that

I'd stopped by. I'd just have to play it off and mention that I put notes in the computer even if he didn't.

I went to the door with her and prepared to smile my way through whatever my father said or did until I could leave.

He blinked when he saw me, then smiled. A genuine smile. "Tallie, I'm so glad you're here. I was hoping Caitlin had someone to talk to."

Who was this and what had he done with my father? Unless he really believed I was going to leave the Hoagie thing alone and thought I was becoming more a part of the funeral home now that Max was going to be helping out? We could be the new power couple of the undertaker set. I wasn't sure I was up for that.

But I knew it would be better to talk with my father at a later time than it would be to take him on right now; that would get me nowhere fast and embarrass the grieving daughter in one fell swoop.

So Dad and I brought Caitlin back into the house and did what we did best together. Talked funerals and clothes and arrangements.

"I'd like him buried in his uniform. He was always so comfortable in that thing, and he loved his store so much." She dabbed at her eyes with a tissue this time, instead of the handkerchief. "Mom had a lovely dress picked out also that I can get from the closet upstairs. I don't think she planned on using it this soon, but at least we have something."

"But we only have Ronda—"

I vehemently shook my head at my father, praying that he'd take my hint and not say anything else.

"Ready, Caitlin. We only have Ronda ready. We'll let you know about Hoagie."

Dad cleared his throat and gave me the side-eye, but he played along, which I couldn't have been more thankful for. "Of course, Caitlin. We can make that happen. I'm sure she'll be stunning." He patted her clasped hands and handed her another tissue from the end table. "Are there any particular songs you'd like played or people you'd like to speak? I'd also be happy to send out any announcements to out-of-town family if you need me to. We don't do that for everyone, but I'm willing to waive the fee for someone who was such an important part of my life for so many years."

Her head snapped up and her eyes went wide. Her gaze darted from left to right over and over again, like she was going to have a seizure or something. I looked at my dad in panic.

"It's okay, Caitlin. You don't have to make any decisions right at this moment. There will be time for that whenever you're ready. Let's stick with the easy things and go from there."

She shook her head so violently the knot on top of her head threatened to fall over or unravel. "No, we don't have any family out of town. We don't know anyone who doesn't live here. We have no one who needs to be contacted and really, I'd rather not, or um, Dad and Mom never wanted an obituary run in the paper, so please don't do that. Don't put it online either." She sounded scared, like a boogeyman was lurking outside her door and it was absolutely imperative that no one outside our small town know that Hoagie and Ronda had passed on to the great big paint shaker in the sky.

I opened my mouth to say something, but my dad gave a short, sharp shake of his head while Caitlin looked at me with pleading eyes. I caught it in my peripheral vision and acknowledged it by patting her hands myself. "No problem, Caitlin. Anything you want is fine. If you'll show me where the clothes are, I can take them with me for when we're ready. If you have a picture of your mom and dad that you'd like us to work from for their final rest, I can also take that."

Caitlin shook her head, softer this time, and said quietly, "Dad didn't let anyone take his picture. I don't even have one from their wedding day. My poor parents . . ."

Chapter Fifteen

Thirty minutes later, I followed my father out the door and to his waiting car. I would have been fine walking back and taking the time to think about all the things I'd learned in that short period of time, but it would look weird if I told him I didn't want him to drive me back to the funeral home when he'd specifically asked to take me there. I wasn't sure what he'd want to talk about, but I was up for whatever he had to say.

My phone pinged a text, and I saw Uncle Sherman wanted to talk to me at the Bean in ten minutes. What could he want and did I have time before dinner at my parents? Just barely, but I'd make it work, I guessed. As soon as I got rid of my dad.

"Thanks for being there, Tallie. I know it's not your favorite thing to do, but I also know you're good at it, and that Caitlin appreciated the presence of another woman."

Words were burning on my tongue, questions I wanted to ask, thoughts I wanted his opinion on. But he would probably have a fit if I admitted I was there to get information instead of giving comfort; that had only been an added bonus for both me and her.

"It's fine, Dad. I do understand how hard it can be for someone to process that the people they loved most in the world are gone."

He blew out a breath. "I don't want to start an argument again, but it's that kind of thing that just makes me baffled as to why you wouldn't want to take your place in the family business. Jeremy's told me how effective you've been with the people you've talked to. You have a smile that lights up the darkest room, and your tone and manner are spot-on for helping those in need. What is it that you hate so much about our business that you'd rather clean houses then work with us? Or is it me? Do you just not want to work with me?"

Oh boy, that was kind of a loaded question, and there were so many answers. Far more than I could go into during the half block we had left before he pulled in behind the home. And I didn't want to sit in the confines of the car and have this discussion when I needed to meet Sherman, then find Burton and find out what in the world he was letting people think.

"It's none of those things, Dad, and yet a piece of all of them. I'm not sure what to tell you, but I have an appointment in a few minutes. Can we talk about this later? It's not that I don't like you, though. I do. I love you. I just . . ." Didn't know what else to say.

He nodded and patted my knee. He was obviously in a patting mood today. Sometimes it was a squeeze to the biceps or a hand stroked over my hair. Today was patting.

"I love you too, honey, and I hope Max will be happy with us for whatever time he can spare, if you both agree on it."

Not that I would ever tell Max what he could or could not do, but I did appreciate my dad saying that without insinuating it would be my fault if Max said no in the end.

"Actually, I think he would be a great addition to the team, and I'm happy to loan him to you for however long he wants to be there or you want him there."

He smiled and I smiled back, feeling for the first time in a long time that we might be on the same wavelength.

I put my hand on the car door and got ready to get out. He squeezed my biceps.

"Before you get out, though, can we talk for a minute about why you were at Caitlin's? Are you going to look into Hoagie's disappearance and Ronda's murder even after I asked you not to?"

I stared straight out the side window and held my breath for ten seconds. That wavelength had been about a two-footer at the shore in Jersey on a winter's day, more like a slight swell than an actual wave.

Now or never, and I guess I was choosing now. "Dad, I'm not sure how to say this either, but this one I'm just going to blurt out. Hoagie was very special to me and I want to find him. I'll repeat myself and say that it's not that I don't think Burton can do his job; I just know that I've helped him ferret out the truth several times now, and I can find out things without all his red tape. Some people don't like to talk to the police, but they'll talk to the cleaner or will talk while ignoring the cleaner. They also say things to someone who asks questions in a non-official capacity, namely me. Plus, something weird is going on. Why does Caitlin think her father is dead instead of just missing? Is Burton letting people believe that Hoagie was actually that corpse outside the store? Why? Aren't you curious as to what he's thinking?"

I looked over my shoulder at him to see if his face was turning red or the vein in his throat was bulging. Instead, it was neither. He looked contemplative, as if he was only listening to understand, not rebuke as soon as I was done talking.

So I continued. I'd already stepped in; I might as well wade around in the water a bit while I was here.

"And the kids aren't happy that Nathan is getting the store. Only one is fine with that. The other three have other ideas of how things should work. One wants to sell, another wants to clean it out and open an art gallery and another wants to rent it out to someone else. They all want something different. Do they think they can contest the will? Are Hoagie's disappearance and Ronda's death related? Is he gone because he killed her? I just want to know."

"I see." Dad rolled his palms over the steering wheel.

"Do you? And why all the secrecy about his life? Why do they have no relatives outside this town? And I can't find them on our family tree. How are they related to us anyway? No one seems to know. Why did Caitlin look like she was in a total panic when you asked, even though she'd just told me that she had an aunt in the south that Hoagie wouldn't let them talk to?"

His brow pulled down between his eyes. That was the classic Bud Graver look of disapproval. I had thought he understood me. Instead, I braced myself for a lecture about staying out of places I wasn't wanted.

"That Burton should be so lucky to have your intuition and your knowledge to help him out. Of course I don't want you to put yourself in danger like you have before, but he would have a number of unsolved cases on his desk and a very bad track record if it hadn't been for you and your willingness to help, even without his consent. I ought to have a word with him."

It took a moment for his words and their meaning to soak into my skull. He was supporting me? He wanted to go talk to Burton like he had one of my teachers who had treated me badly in third grade just because she had not liked my aunt when she'd taught her years before and thought to take it out on me?

I laughed and laughed, and then I turned in his big old Cadillac to give him a huge and fierce hug. "I love you, Dad. You talking to Burton is not going to help anyone, but I so appreciate your support and the very thought that you would take him on for me. You're the best. I've got this, though. And I'm not going to try to hand him clues this time as they come up. I'm going to solve the whole thing, then package it like a present and hand it to him with a huge bow on it, all without getting myself in trouble at all. What he does with it from that point will be up to him and will have nothing to do with me."

"That's my girl. Tenacity, that should have been your middle name instead of Beverly."

This time he stroked his hand over my hair, then kissed me on the cheek. "I wondered about the Hoagie thing myself but didn't want to correct her in case it had to do with her grief. If you need anything, let me know, and I'll see if I can dig into the archives. I have his information in a file from years ago, before we went digital. I didn't throw anything away, just in case the computers went down one day and we needed something. They're in the basement and might take a little time to get into, but as soon as I find them, they're yours. Get whoever did this to Ronda and find Hoagie, Tallie, and make it stick."

After that, there wasn't much more to say and I practically floated out of the car. I didn't know what had just happened or why my dad had so completely changed his tune, but I wasn't going to question it. We'd spent years with me feeling either like I never was enough or was too much, so having his support like this was a whole new experience.

I glanced at my watch. Okay, this was an experience I'd have to enjoy later. I had forty-five minutes to find Sherman, then go after and berate Burton before I had to get home and be ready to eat dinner with my parents and the dragon lady.

So as not to test out the new flush of feeling supported, I waited for my dad to leave in his car again before I hopped across the street. He might be on board with the Hoagie thing, but I didn't know if he'd be so understanding of my desire to drill Burton for answers.

I sent a quick text to Max to see if he could start digging up anything on the four Hogart kids or find anything more than I had on Ronda and Hoagie. I'd meant to ask him earlier, but everyone seemed to need a piece of my time and I was running out of it.

Drinks and pie were just being set down at a small table in the back of the Bean when I walked through the door.

Peanut butter pie and a cup of steaming coffee with enough cream to make it blond. Did he know, or did Gina just set down what she knew I'd want?

That was the least of my questions when I saw all the paperwork Sherman had laid out across the small table.

"You should've asked for a four topper instead of a two," I said as I sat down.

"Meh, most of this is duplicate information. I just wanted to make sure I had everything I wanted to give you."

I was a little blown away. Okay, I lied; I was a lot blown away. I had just expected to come in, get the low-down on what he thought might be going on and then be sent on my way to create my own kind of chaos. This looked very organized and methodical. I typically wasn't either of those. I seriously hoped I didn't disappoint him.

"This is a . . . lot."

"Bah, don't be put off by it. Each fire has a ton of reports that have to be filled out and filed and then done again in triplicate. I just want you to have everything you could possibly need."

"Okay."

He finally looked up from shuffling the mountains of paperwork. "Girlie, don't even start getting those cold feet. You're going to love this, and any amount of help is going to be much appreciated, even if you only look over what I have and see something I haven't seen before. I'm not asking for a miracle, though I certainly wouldn't turn one down. I just need a new set of eyes and ears, and you've got some of the best out there."

"You can stop with all the flattery, it's just you and me here. And you no longer have to try to convince me."

His eyes squinted almost shut and his lips flattened into a straight line. "I'm going to say this once, and it's not because you're my favorite niece, though you'd better not ever repeat that. And it's not because I want or need your help. It's not even because you're one of my favorite people and I'm so thankful you're back after all those years of removing yourself from us. So listen up when I tell you that you are one smart cookie, Tallulah Beverly Graver. Burton won't see it and Waldo tried to crush it, and your dad doesn't understand your brand of smart. But I do, and Max does, and I think you are awesome."

It had been a while since I'd truly blushed, but I felt one rising right then. No silly compliments, no jokes, no qualifiers, just acceptance and acknowledgment and love. And I might have cried if it wasn't for the fact that Burton walked in at that very moment.

Chapter Sixteen

"Why do I get the feeling you're having a let's-hate-Burton meeting?" He peered between Sherman and me with his hands on his hips and his feet spread wide. His stance wasn't aggressive necessarily, just weary.

And this is why I always wanted to help him. Because he was a good guy and we had had so few murders in town until the past few years. And when things didn't get solved quickly, he was the one to blame. But he'd un-equivocally told me to butt out before and this time it was different. I didn't hate him, but I did need to know what he was thinking, or if he had let Caitlin believe her father was dead or specifically told her he was. I was not going to go against his story if possible, but I needed to know what it was before I tried to skirt around it.

"Burton," Sherman said gruffly. He made a show of gathering all his paperwork and stacking it neatly into two piles. Then he turned it over, folded his hands over it and stared straight at the chief of police.

I wasn't quite that bold, so I sat on my hands and said, "Hi, Burton. We aren't having any kind of meeting like that. If you're looking for Mama Shirley, I think she's at home watching one of her soaps." I looked around for Gina, who hadn't yet appeared, even though she had to have heard someone had come in the front door. "I'm sure Gina will be out in a minute, or I can get you something started?"

"It's fine. I'll wait while the two of you have your powwow, and then you can go back to talking about me when I'm gone."

Sherman harrumphed. "You know the whole world does not revolve around you, man. Tallie and I are talking a different kind of business. I have that firebug running around and I need to find him. I know you're working on it too, but neither of us are getting anywhere. Tallie always seems to have her ear to the ground, so I thought I'd ask for her help in finding out anything I possibly can to do my job."

The implication there was that Burton wasn't smart enough to do that. He caught it like a blow, rocking back a step. "You know, it's actually my job, Sherman, but I hope she can help both of us. She's helped a lot before, even without me asking. I'm sure she'll do just fine with our arsonist."

Now I was more confused than ever. He admitted I'd helped, was letting Sherman know he had chosen wisely, and yet I knew without a single doubt that if I told him I had questions about his methods with Hoagie's pseudo-death right now, he'd shut me down faster than a vacuum that had gone haywire.

So I didn't ask. I just sat there as Gina finally emerged from the back, her hair a little mussed and a huge smile on her face.

Jeremy tried to sneak out the side, but I caught him and called him over.

His sigh was big enough to blow a couple of napkins off the counter. "What, Tallie?"

"Hey, big brother, just wanted to see if we have anything going on tomorrow? Sherman has asked for my help, and I thought I'd see what the schedule is like."

His look was skeptical, but I kept up the chatter just in case he was going to say something to contradict the good feelings I had going on, with compliments from both Sherman and Burton floating around my head.

"No, nothing new. Ronda should be released in a day or so, and then the real work will begin. With Max on board, I don't think we'll need you for anything but helping with the service or driving the hearse. I know how much you like driving that thing."

I didn't know if "like" was quite the right word, but the goodwill seemed to be flowing in the coffee shop, and I didn't want to contradict him. "Sounds good. Just let me know when you need me."

"Sure thing. See you later." He looked back over his shoulder and gave a wave to his new fiancée. Was I ready for them to be married? I guess it was the wrong time to ask that question, considering it was already in the works.

Burton got his to-go cup and started to head out again with a brief wave and no further conversation. His shoulders drooped when he got to the door, and it took everything I had not to run after him.

But I wasn't going to do that. Sherman cleared his throat to get my attention. "He'll be fine."

"No, I'm not sure this is one of those okay times." I turned in my chair. "Burton, do you have a moment?"

He took his hand from the door knob but didn't look at us.

"Come on. I just have a few questions, and this way I don't have to find you later. We can get it all out of the way now, so you don't have to deal with me twice in one day."

A derisive chuckle was the only response I got for a moment, and then he came back to the table with a half-smile. "You know, it's really not that bad to deal with you."

"Three compliments from three men in an hour. I don't know if I can handle this much goodwill. I know it's Christmastime and everything, but my head might explode."

Both he and Sherman laughed. The tension left Burton for just a second. It came right back, but at least there had been that blip in time.

"What do you need to know?" he asked. He took a sip of his coffee, and I was kind enough to wait for him to swallow it before I hit him with the big guns. I didn't want him to spit it out on me.

"Why do Hoagie's children think he's dead when you and I know that's not true?"

He sputtered anyway, but at least there was nothing in his mouth except the teeth he bared at me. "What did you say?"

"Does she really have to repeat herself, Burton? I'm thinking you heard the question the first time and are just buying time to figure out why you'd do that to a family who was already grieving their mother's death." Sherman sat back in his chair of judgment, while I leaned forward to be able to keep my voice down.

"Are you letting them think that, hoping Hoagie will come out of the woodwork if everyone thinks he's dead?"

"Don't give him excuses, girlie. Let him think up his own lie."

"Sherman . . ." I looked at him with what I hoped was censure in my gaze.

"What?"

"Back down."

"Fine, but I'm interested to hear what he's come up with now that you gave him some extra time."

Burton placed his cup on our table, then leaned forward with his hands planted firmly on either side of it. "First of all, I don't need time to come up with a lie because I have no intention of lying." Burton moved his cup on top of Sherman's paperwork and pulled up another chair. He leaned in, and Sherman and I leaned in with him. "I didn't tell anyone that Hoagie was dead. Who did you talk to?"

Could he really not know? "Caitlin. I went by the house today on official funeral home business, and she had outfits all picked out for her mother and her father. She's convinced he's dead. I didn't correct her in the moment. I was afraid I'd set her off, and I wasn't sure if it was a story she was telling herself to explain away his disappearance. It's bad form to mess with the grieving until they've had a little time to face facts."

"Interesting. You're good at that, girlie." Sherman smiled when I glared at him. He raised his hands as if in surrender. "I'm just saying, the apple didn't fall far from the tree, even if it's often trying to find someone to roll it down the hill or carry it away, as the case may be."

I rolled my eyes because I was not going to tell him my dad had said pretty much the same thing.

"Let's get back to the point." I turned my cup around and around, wishing it had answers I just couldn't see yet. "Do all the kids think their father is dead? Caitlin was saying they're already squabbling over the will, so they must."

"I have no idea, but no one has said anything to me about this."

"See, she always gets that insider info that no one else seems to get. She's a whiz."

"We don't need to go that far. People just seem to think they can talk to me without repercussions." I shook my head. "So, Burton, do you think one of them brought that body up from West Virginia? Were you able to look into that?"

"I put Matt on it, Tallie, but he hasn't figured anything out yet. We don't know what the connection is, or how someone found an almost duplicate of Hoagie. I'd really like to find the man myself and ask more than a few questions, but he's either long gone or an expert at hiding."

After pulling a pen from my bag, I made a quick note on a napkin. "Have you been able to talk with Nathan? Caitlin says he's the one who inherits the store if Hoagie and Ronda die, but only if Ronda died first, because she was fighting Hoagie tooth and nail about it, according to the youngest, Chrissy."

"But how does this all tie in?" Burton asked the question but seemed more to be talking to himself. Not for long, though. "What are your thoughts, Tallie?"

I didn't even know what to say. I had so many, but they were all half-formed. "Did someone kill Ronda and then the kids thought it was a good time for Hoagie to go too? But that doesn't make a ton of sense, because why would they kill him without getting the will changed first? Or did they kill Ronda too? But why? Something had to have happened to set all this in motion."

"I don't know either, and I've come to the same conclusions. We have to find Hoagie, the real one." Burton's face pulled into a tight frown.

"Agreed," I said. "And Ronda's killer. And the arsonist. Do you think they have anything to do with one another?" That thought had just popped into my head, but I couldn't see how it would make sense because the fires started before the Ronda thing.

"It would be a lot easier if they did, but the timing is off." Burton stood. "I have to go see how Matt is doing with the info I gave him, and then I'm calling it a night for now. Let me know if you find anything, Tallie. Sherman, we'll talk later about any ideas you have. No matter what you think of me, I'd never shut you out if you have information you think will help. I want this firebug caught just as much as you do, if not more."

When Burton left, Uncle Sherman and I looked at each other.

"Do you think the two of you will ever get over your feud? It was a ton of years ago and she's gone from both your lives," I said.

He snorted. "It's not just that. We've had animosity since we were little. He just rubs me wrong, and I do the same for him. But we can put that aside for the moment to do the right thing. Now, let's look at what I brought you."

"Hey, before we get into that, do you know how Hoagie is related to us?"

"Well . . ." Sherman looked at the hammered tin ceiling and rubbed his chin. "Isn't he your uncle, or maybe he's your dad's uncle? Or your mom's? I can't keep track of everyone all the time. Our tree's roots are about as deep as you can get around here, almost more than Gina's, but don't tell her mom that."

I laughed. "It'll be our secret." Then I sobered up. "You know, the funny thing is that no one can seem to remember exactly how Hoagie is related. Even Mama Shirley went to her own genealogy, and he isn't there. And when she tried to talk to one of the cousins, she didn't know either. It's like someone just started calling him uncle one day, and we all fell into line."

"Hmmm. Well, whatever it is, it's a done deal at the moment and I need you on this. Can I count on you to help me, Tallie?"

The difference between dealing with Burton and dealing with Sherman was immense. And yet I felt far more pressure to please my uncle than when I was defying Burton. Call me crazy, but I almost liked when I could surprise Burton with tidbits, instead of having someone depend on me to bring in the answers.

"Of course," I said despite my reservations. "I'll take the info and go over it with Max, if that's okay. Maybe between the two of us, we'll see something that is being missed."

"I sure hope so." He flipped the paperwork back over. "We've had five suspicious fires in four weeks and that's four too many if someone is setting them instead of it just being the old knob and tube wiring that still exists in some of these houses."

After that, we got down to business. Max came over about ten minutes into it and pulled up the chair Burton had put back when he'd left. Sherman went back over what we'd already covered. Basically, an accelerant was used in all five fires. Some kind of chemical that started the fire, along with matches or a lighter. There were no bombs, no fragments of something going off, just houses where no one happened to be home going up in flames. The damage was mainly interior, the charred insides black as night, but little damage on the outside of the buildings. So that meant that the fire was inside the house. And then a person—refusing to give a name, only the address where the fire was—called the fire station and then hung up.

Or that was what had happened at the beginning. Sherman was worried now about the business fire.

"Wow, Sherman, this is some nasty business if you think these are deliberate," Max said.

"Yeah, you're telling me. I don't know what they're after, because the fire cleanup guys have checked the contents of the house they've been able to save with each family, and nothing is missing that they can tell. So it's not a burglary they're trying to cover up. No one seems to have anything in common, like jobs, family, part of some civic organization with enemies. I tried all the triggers and nothing is popping."

"Do the police have anything else?" I asked, flipping the pages over one by one while I skimmed the information.

"Not really, because as of yet, there's not much to go on. No one has been hurt, and nothing has been stolen, so there's not a lot to look at besides the actual fire."

"That's got to be frustrating." Max took the pages I'd already looked over and scanned them himself. "We'll see if we can find anything."

"I'd appreciate it." Sherman rose from his chair. "I gotta head out. Tell your mom I might be late to dinner tonight, but go on without me. I'm on call and it's been a heck of a day since the last fire. Who knows when another will come up? They seem to be getting closer together, and I don't like it. I don't want that one fire where someone does get hurt to happen and we could have avoided it if I'd just looked closer."

He shook Max's hand and hugged me before walking out the front door. Gina swooped in on us as soon as the door closed behind him.

"What have you gotten yourself into now, Tallie?"

"Don't you start."

She had the gall to laugh. "I'm not going to reprimand you. I just want to know if it's something I can help with. You guys all looked so serious. Then Burton lingered longer than he normally does, so I didn't want to interrupt. Can I help?"

"Keep your ears open for anyone who might be setting fires." I shrugged after that. "I don't know what more we can do. And no matter what else is happening, I'm also listening for anything having to do with Ronda's death and Hoagie's disappearance. So this will just have to ride tandem."

I hoped I hadn't taken on more than I could handle.

Chapter Seventeen

Dinner tonight was different from Christmas. For one thing, it was only Grams, Dad, Mom, Max and me. Sherman had bowed out at the last second when a call had come into the station. It wasn't a fire, so that was at least something, but he'd be working late again.

I spaced myself away from Grams by a few chairs and waited with anticipation for the meat loaf to be delivered to the table. We were on the snowflake plates again, but this felt less festive. My dad would need to go right after it was done to get back to work. A natural death had come yesterday and was on the table, Hoagie's near twin was still in the basement, even though the funeral guy from West Virginia would probably want him back at some point if the widow returned to pay, and Ronda was there ready to be worked on. He'd have a lot of hours over the next few days. Max would be working next to him and getting an idea of what was entailed in being a funeral director.

I was still trying to wrap my head around that. Not the working with my dad part, but what he'd actually be doing.

As I sat still waiting for the meat loaf with my salivary glands doing three times their normal work, Dad was trying to talk him into going back to school to get the parts of a degree he'd need to have to prepare the bodies.

"The schooling's not that bad, and you already have a lot of credits, so they should count toward anything you need in the general ed section."

Max, to his credit, shook his head. "Let's see if this works out first before we start getting me to the stage where I'm emptying people and filling them up with embalming fluid."

Grams shook her head. "Is that truly appropriate conversation for the table? I'm pretty sure we can come up with some other topic that doesn't involve disemboweling people."

I snickered into my water glass as Dad frowned. "Now, Jane, we weren't talking about the details, only that I'd like Max to consider being a full mortician."

"And you might just want to consider yourself lucky he wants to learn to be a funeral director. Get him hooked on that first before you start pulling him into the darker side of what you do." She sniffed. "Pass the green beans, please."

Dad frowned and Mom just blushed.

"So, Grams, how is your visit going so far?" When she'd contacted my mother to let her know she would be gracing us with her presence, my mom was very clear that it was my job to step in to save her from her mom whenever possible. And I'd been neglecting that job recently in my pursuit of all the weird things that had been happening with the death of Ronda and the disappearance of Hoagie. I hadn't done one shopping excursion with them or a single lunch. Grams was still going to be here through the New Year, so it wasn't like I didn't have time, but I felt like I was falling down on the job at the moment.

"Well, between the death of Cousin Ronda and then the way Hoagie left this earth, I can't say it's been the best of times, but at least your mother has been attentive."

"Oh, Tallie has been busy. Hopefully, we'll be able to get together soon, and she was able to make both dinners, so that's been appreciated. She also went to bingo, if you remember."

And there was my mom jumping in to my defense. I wished she didn't have to do that, but I'd take it at the moment, and I'd see her one chip to throw down on the table because I could change the subject in a heartbeat.

"Grams, how is Hoagie related to us?" I speared my fork into a nice-sized bite of meat loaf, dipped it in ketchup and shoved it in my mouth. I wasn't going to tell her why I wanted to know unless she refused to answer without the information, but I found it easier to have my mouth full at the moment. That way I didn't run off with reasons when I should just wait her out. Or try to find out why she also thought Hoagie was dead.

"Well, that's an interesting question, Tallie. Why do you want to know?"

I chewed the rest of the way through the melt-in-my-mouth meat loaf before answering. "Just making conversation." I prayed my father wouldn't look up from his plate to tell on me for my lie.

"Conversation. I don't think so. Try again, young lady."

I looked around the ceiling and then at all the knick-knacks my mother had displayed in the dining room to come up with inspiration. Nothing came to me, though. I decided to stay as close to the truth as possible so I didn't get into trouble with a lie that made no sense. But I didn't get a chance.

"We were talking about lineages in town with all of this mayhem around here, and it came up," Max said, verbally stepping between me and Grams. "Tallie remembers calling him uncle, but not how he's related, so I encouraged her to ask you."

"Ha! Don't try to save her, young man. I know a lie when I hear one. She can tell me why she really wants to know, and we'll go from there, or I'm not answering."

I looked up from my plate to find her eyes narrowed and her gaze zeroed in on me. Seriously, it could just have been a question to make conversation. I knew of course that it wasn't, but that didn't mean she should. On the other hand, it was always easier to come out and tell her than try to skirt around the woman who'd had to deal with my aunt Diane, who now lived in North Carolina. That woman had known every trick in the book and still hadn't gotten anything by Grams.

I put my elbows on the table and ignored my mother's murmured admonishment.

"Here's the truth. Something is going on in town. Some people think Ronda was killed by Hoagie, who then went into hiding. I find it hard to believe that the man would put up with her crap for all these years only to clock her in the head with one of his own varnish cans on Christmas Eve after bingo. I was the one who realized that the body outside the hardware store was not in fact

Hoagie, and yet his kids seem to think it is him and he's dead. To be honest, I want to know how he was related to us so I can look into other things."

"Very well, but first, why are you looking into this when Burton is more than capable, as well as my grandson, Matthew? I don't believe they need you meddling into something that has nothing to do with you. And, frankly, I'm surprised your father hasn't forbidden you to take on something like this, especially with how horrible the other cases have gone, from what I've heard."

So it was going to be the ladies who tried to tear me down today and the men who boosted me up. Interesting. But I faced off against her anyway. It wasn't like she could do anything to me that I didn't let her. And maybe always staying under her radar had not been in my best interest.

It hadn't exactly worked for my mother.

"I want my town to be safe, and if there's anything I can do to help, I do it."

"It sounds dangerous and ridiculous to me. Like a vigilante. Years ago, a woman's place was taking care of her husband, standing behind his dreams and ambitions to help him make them come true. While I didn't subscribe to that entirely, you've gone too far off the path."

Oh my word! What century were we living in?

"I'd have to respectfully disagree with you on that, ma'am." Max slid back into the conversation. "Tallie is very good at what she does: cleaning, sleuthing and helping at the funeral home. I wouldn't want her to give up everything she does to make sure that my dreams come true. I want hers to come true too. And I'd do anything I could to ensure that happens."

Wow. And I wasn't the only one thinking that, because

Mom sat with her mouth slightly open and my dad had a little smile on his face that disappeared as soon as Grams looked at him.

She slapped a hand on the table and laughed. "I like this one much better than that Waldo creep. I'm not sure what you ever saw in him except an avenue to escape all of this." She waved her hand around. "And look at you now. You'd better keep this one."

"I'll toast to that," Mom said, lifting her glass of iced tea.

"You don't need to do any more toasting, Karen." My grandmother took the glass out of her hand and put it down. "I think you've probably had enough."

But Mom hadn't had anything, unless she wasn't sharing the good stuff with the rest of us.

Grams took it back to us before I could ask why I wasn't given access to the wine. "I'll tell you how he's related, and then you go find out what happened. This is one of our own, and we don't leave that to just anyone to take care of. Matt is doing a great job, I'm sure, but even he might need a little help. I would suggest any information you find you give to him instead of Burton, though, so that your cousin can get that promotion he's been looking for."

"I can try to do that, but I've been working directly with Burton."

"Maybe it's time you changed that."

I made no commitment to that, although if I did give everything to Matt from now on, it could look like I wasn't involved at all and would take me out of Burton's laser vision in the future. Even though he was asking for my help this time, he normally didn't. He could come to his senses at any moment. Of course I wasn't sure Burton would believe I was staying out of things after he'd asked for my help. Plus, how would it look if Matt was suddenly bursting with information he couldn't explain where he'd gotten?

"I'll think about it. Now, how's Hoagie related to us?"

"The truth is, he's not."

"Wait. What?" My mom sat forward in her chair with a look of total and complete disbelief on her face. "That can't be true."

"Oh, but it is."

"But . . ." I started, then stopped to gather my thoughts. "But he came to all of our family picnics and reunions. We've always called him uncle. His kids were my cousins, even if we've grown apart and I don't have much to do with them."

Grams wiped the corners of her mouth with a napkin before zeroing in on me. "We adopted him and his family, at the request of Burton's father. I'm not sure why Hal chose us instead of taking him and his family on for himself. Their tree would have been big enough to hide him better in the branches, but for some reason, Burton Senior came to your grandfather before you were born and asked if we could graft him on to our family tree."

"Why, though?" I was absolutely baffled. It was one thing to have friends for so long that they felt like family. Or friends that were so dear as to be family, like Gina and Mama Shirley. But actually taking someone and their family in and passing them off as relatives seemed strange, especially when it was a request from Burton's father.

"I don't actually know. After being approached by Hal, your grandfather, God rest his soul, asked, and I said yes. We started everyone calling him Uncle Hoagie and her Aunt Ronda. They already had Caitlin and Carl—Calvin and Chrissy came after they'd been here for a few years. And then they just melted in with us."

"How did you explain it? Do you know where they came from before they arrived in town? Were they hiding from something?" The bafflement continued and spewed more questions.

"I didn't question it. I wasn't raised to question, which is one of the reasons I thought I raised your mother to be more independent."

Ow, that was a dig, and now I was going to be the one defending. "My mother is a wonderful person who is very independent. And she makes the best snickerdoodles ever."

Grams scoffed. "Snickerdoodles from my great-grandmother's recipe, and that shouldn't be your only life accomplishment."

Mom's shoulders dropped farther and farther with every word, as if she were being physically crushed instead of just emotionally. I didn't know what else I could say or do, though, to make my grandmother stop her tirade.

"It's a shame you feel that way, ma'am. I feel that Mrs. Graver is one of the biggest reasons I not only graduated high school but went on to excel at both college and as a government employee. If it weren't for her, I might have gotten lost in the gangs in DC. It might not be saving the world, but it saved mine, and that's something I will forever be grateful for." Max for the save again. How did he always know what to say and how to say it? I'd have to remember that if we ever got around to actually fighting. I might fall short on the arguing scale if that was what I had to contend with.

I squeezed his hand under the table. Mom wiped her eyes and smiled at him. Grams scowled at first, then finally broke into a real smile. "Oh my, this one is a real keeper. Nothing like your grandfather and very much like your father. Good job there, Tallie."

And just like that, the tension decreased. I still would have liked her to apologize to my mother, but I had a feeling that that might happen at a later date, because Grams took my mother's hand on top of the table and patted it. "You did a good job with them, Karen."

And Max was going to be an awesome funeral director, with his forthright but compassionate take on things. Guess I'd better settle into the idea of being a funeral director's significant other. There were worse things.

The rest of dinner went on without a hitch. We talked a bit about the murders, but no one had anything solid to offer. Dad had gotten in touch with the director from West Virginia and had agreed to mentor the poor guy once things calmed down over here. He'd also found out that the widow was still missing.

So more questions, but also some answers. I'd take it, if that was all I was going to get. Now I had to get in touch with Burton to find out why he hadn't told me that Hoagie wasn't actually related to us, and if he knew why his father had asked my grandfather to lie for all these years. Were Hoagie and his family hiding in plain sight? Was that why he didn't want Ronda calling out of state, and why Caitlin looked like she was going to pass out when my father asked about out-of-town relatives?

I felt behind the ball and left out in the rain, but I'd ask before I assumed. Maybe that would work better than my usual methods.

It was late, so I called Matt to see what the situation was before trying Burton on his cell.

"Ah, Tallie, the woman of the hour. How are things with the investigation? Should I ask you who the actual murderer is so that we can close the case?"

"Hello to you too, cousin of mine. Grams asked after you tonight and wants to know when she might be seeing you while she's here through the New Year."

He groaned. "Do you think I could get away with just telling her that I'm always on night shift and have crazy hours?"

"I think she'd tan your hide and make you take her out to an expensive restaurant with seven-course meals to lengthen your time together when she finally did catch you."

He laughed and I continued. "Seriously, if you just stop in at my mom's for a few minutes, I bet that would be plenty. And then she'll be gone, maybe for another couple of years. You can do this. I had to. Twice for dinner with the dragon lady. Pull up those big girl panties and bite the bullet, dear cousin."

"Biting the bullet might be what I want to do right about now. There is so much going on, and as much as I was ribbing you about solving the murder, I wouldn't be against you having some kind of information. Burton and I are both at a loss. Nothing's connecting in either investigation. We have a dead citizen, a corpse transported over state lines, a missing store owner who has to be tied to both of them in some way we aren't seeing and the ever-present arsonist. I feel like I'm in a tornado that is most definitely not carrying me off to the Land of Oz."

"Where is Burton? I have a few questions for him my-self."

"Anything I can help with?" he asked.

"I have no idea. There's so much going on that I don't know where to start. Did you find out anything about that corpse?"

"Nothing. I can't seem to find out much except that he was in jail for almost forty years for a murder. They tried him for drug trafficking too, but those charges were dropped when they got him for murder. It doesn't connect to anything in our town that I can see, though, and no rea-son why his body would be here. I don't know much more than that, but I can page Burton for you if you need him."

A novel idea, but not one that would get me the imme-diate answer I wanted, and it was getting late. "I was going to just call his cell."

"That thing has been blowing up all night. Paging him might be your better bet. Mind if I tag along for a meetup?"

"Not at all. Actually, it might be infinitely better if you're there."

Max came up behind me just as I hung up with Matt. "So, you'll be out and about tonight even though it's get-ting late?" He put his arms around my waist and rested his chin on the top of my head. "Should I be worried? Do you need me to come with you?"

"I think you've earned a night off for once. You did a lot today, and I can't thank you enough for standing up to my grandmother for my mom."

"Hey, all in a day's work, and I've always thought of her as a mom, and it will be official when we eventually get married."

Married. It was sounding better and better, and I could deal with the mortician stuff if it came to be. But first, I had to get to Burton to find out what he knew.

My phone rang. Matt was back quickly. That could be good or it could be bad.

"He says to meet him at the diner in ten minutes."

"The diner? Why can't I just meet him at the station? I'm so full after dinner and I'm going to feel bad if I don't order something."

"Well, he hasn't eaten yet and he said he figured he should be sitting down for whatever news you're going to hit him with."

Well, this ought to be fun.

Chapter Eighteen

In the end, I chose to bring Max with me, even though he'd promised to meet my dad in the basement tomorrow bright and early for his first lesson on doing a dead person's hair and makeup.

We both sat on the right side of a booth waiting for Burton to arrive. I did order a chocolate milk and a slice of pumpkin pie, although I just took tiny bites every time the waitress walked by and had no intention of actually eating the whole thing.

Max didn't have the same qualms and chose a bowl of Italian wedding soup and pretty much sucked it right down.

"Tell me you weren't still hungry after all that meat loaf."

He rubbed his stomach. "Not too hungry, but maybe

it's the climate or the air or my contentment. I guess I'm just hungry. I'm going to have to watch it, though, if I still want to fit into my clothes."

We were still laughing when Burton made a beeline for us from the front counter, bypassing the waitress, who tried to lead him to the table.

"Let's make this quick. Things are happening, and I'm starving." As if on cue, a Reuben sandwich arrived at the table. Burton almost shoved half the sandwich into his mouth with his first bite.

I waited for him to swallow for the second time today. "Tell me what you know about Hoagie not actually being a part of my family, but your father asking my grand-parents to fake that he was a limb on our tree from days gone by."

He must still have had some food in his mouth because he swallowed hard. So hard I could see his Adam's apple strain over something in his throat. "What?" The word came out strangled.

I really hoped I wasn't going to have to perform the Heimlich maneuver.

"You okay?" Max asked.

"Yeah, yeah, fine," Burton croaked. "Give me a min-ute and some water."

I moved my glass across the table because I hadn't taken a sip from it yet, then waited for Burton to get him-self back under control. Either he was surprised I'd found out and was trying to figure out how to continue to lie to me, or he really hadn't known and would have some questions for his dad.

Burton cleared his throat a few times and took a deep

breath. "Okay, let's start again." He took out that little notebook from his pocket and flipped to the next tattered page. I should have gotten him a new one for his birthday, or Christmas, or both. It still wasn't too late to do that.

I put it on my mental list of things to do after all the other little things, and then moved forward with my question again.

"So, my grandmother tells me that Hoagie isn't actually a part of our family. Your father asked my grandfather to pretend he was related to us over forty years ago, and my grandfather agreed. They introduced him as a long-lost cousin from out of town, though my grandmother doesn't remember from where, and they perpetuated the lie up until this very day. So, what do you know about that?"

Burton was scribbling furiously in his notebook, so I assumed he had not known, unless he was fabricating a lie and just doodling until I stopped talking. But he stopped his scribbling and peered at me with one eye squinted.

"Is that all?"

"I'm not sure what more you want, but my mom is looking into some papers to see if there are any letters or pictures of Hoagie, because no one seems to have any, and Caitlin said that her parents were always scared. Maybe they were scared of being found? And remember that Chrissy got in huge trouble for leaving the state. She said they weren't even allowed to go to the mall by themselves. Apparently, her parents took stranger danger to a new level. So maybe someone they were running from finally found them."

More furious scribbling.

"Is it possible to find out if there are any old police stories about them? I looked on the internet and saw nothing but things about the store, and none of those had any Hoagie pictures, except for the one with him dressed up as Santa, where you wouldn't be able to tell who he was anyway. And even in this day and age, Max didn't find anything on social media or on the internet in general on any of them. How are we supposed to catch people doing bad things if they don't tell all on the internet?"

Burton smiled, just a small one at my joke, but then got serious. "I can look, but I already had Matt on that and he said he didn't find anything either." Burton looked down at the notepad and flipped a few pages back and forth.

"What about the corpse? Did that pan out as anything? Matt says the deceased was in jail for murder and then died shortly after he was released."

He flipped back two more pages. "Nothing. The funeral director isn't a whole lot of fun to talk to, and he refused to give me anything except the name and the fact that the widow is still missing."

More people walked into the diner, and we all stopped talking to check them out. I'd been trying to keep my voice down; not everyone needed to know everything we were talking about. And if Burton still wanted everyone to think Hoagie was dead, I didn't want to blow his cover. Speaking of that . . .

"What's the deal with letting Hoagie's kids think he's dead? Why haven't you told them it's a fake?"

He rubbed his forehead. "You are just full of questions."

"I'd rather be full of answers, but you have more than I do, and you're not sharing. I almost flubbed that story this afternoon when I went to see Caitlin and she told me that she had an outfit all picked out for dear old dad."

"I never told Caitlin her dad was dead. She didn't bring it up to me at all. That could mean that she is part of bringing up the corpse and thinks she snowed us all. Or it could mean that she really has no clue. I honestly don't know which theory to go with anymore."

"I don't know any more than you do. I have plans to see if I can get with Carl or Calvin soon to see what their views are on the whole thing. Right now, I have one sister who's fine with not inheriting and one that is angry enough to spit and blaming Nathan. I think she might just be jealous that Nathan and Jenna are going to inherit everything and Hoagie's kids get nothing."

"But they can't inherit at all if we don't find Hoagie."

I bit my lip. "Good point. So, do you think Caitlin is pretending Hoagie is dead so that the will can be read and they can all move forward? But what does she get out of it? Unless somehow she'll get a kickback from the store? But then that would implicate Nathan, wouldn't it? And he was at the register when the sprinklers went off right before the Hoagie double was found."

"That's also a possibility. And that's part of the issue. Too many damn possibilities. We need to narrow them down."

"You're avoiding my question. Why aren't you telling those kids that their dad isn't dead and in my basement?"

I crossed my arms and sat back against the booth. Max stayed with his hands folded on the table, just taking in our conversation like a ping-pong match.

"Can I insert something here?" he finally asked.

Burton and I both looked at him.

"Sure," I said, just as Burton said, "Why not?"

I rolled my eyes and waited for Max to speak.

"So, you have a dead woman, an already dead guy and a missing widow and a missing husband to the dead woman."

I nodded.

"Do you think it could be some kind of conspiracy for Hoagie to run away with the widow? Maybe they orchestrated this, and now they're going to ride off into the sunset together and live happily ever after?"

I gave it some consideration. Burton appeared to do the same thing.

"But why would they make such a big production of it, and why that close to home?" Burton asked. "They could have killed Ronda somewhere other than the firehouse steps, or made it look like an accident in the hardware store. Like tip a whole shelf of paint on her head, or have her get cut by a runaway chainsaw. Why outside bingo on Christmas Eve with a can from Hoagie's store?"

Max shrugged. "I have no idea. I just feel like everything is connected in some way that we're just not seeing. Are there any new people in town who aren't accounted for?"

"There're too many relatives in town for me to know that for sure, and with this firebug thing, I'm out looking at everyone I know and don't know. We might be a small town, but I don't know everyone on a first-name basis."

When the waitress came by to refill our drinks, we stopped talking again. I had time to think and came up with an idea Burton was going to hate, but I had to throw it out there anyway.

"I think we should ask your dad about Hoagie first, and then see where the rest of it falls into place after that."

As I knew would happen, Burton blanched and put down his glass of soda without taking a drink. "I'll look in the police archives and also my dad's journals. If he really asked that of your grandfather, there should be some kind of information or paperwork detailing what happened and why. My dad was incredibly thorough back in his day,"

He was still incredibly thorough to my knowledge, but he lived in a home now. And he and Burton hadn't spoken in years because Burton had put him there when it became obvious he could no longer take care of himself. Sherman had been called out a number of times for fires in the old man's house, and the older Burton had fallen four times before the younger one had finally had to make the decision to move him from the house his family had owned for generations.

I hadn't been around for that because I'd been up on the hill, married to Waldo, but even I had heard about the fight that had lasted days and involved much throwing of breakable things. My gaze zeroed in on Burton's eyebrow, where a scar stood out white. His father had struck him with the urn his mother had been put in after her death. It was not something anyone talked about anymore. I didn't want to bring it up now, but I felt it was absolutely imperative that we talk to Burton Senior, and as soon as possible.

I willed Max not to ask any questions because he didn't know the situation. I didn't want him to step into a quagmire when things were actually going pretty well up until this point.

It was time for me to take one for the team. "I'll go talk to your dad. I can tell him that I'm doing genealogy work and need to know the truth about Hoagie. He might not buy it, but then again, he might, and I think that's a chance we have to take."

The stoicism on Burton's face made my heart hurt, but we had to get the information. And if I took on this task, I'd save Burton the trouble, as well as freeing up his time to look into other things, like who this widow was and if there was indeed a conspiracy of the lovey-dovey kind.

"Fine. Fine, talk to him, but if you're smart, you won't mention me at all. He still throws things when it comes to hearing my name, and he's not going to want to have anything to do with helping me. He and your grandfather used to be best friends, so that should be enough to get you in the door, at least."

"Understood. It's late now, so I'll talk with him tomorrow and let you know if I find out anything."

He shoved the last piece of his sandwich in his mouth, then wiped his mouth with the paper napkin at his elbow. "I'll talk to you later."

He rose from the table and walked out without looking at anyone, even those who waved to him.

"Wow, I don't think I've ever seen Burton like that." Max looked around for the waitress, who came right over. "We'll just get the check and then head out. I think he forgot to pay."

"Nah, he has a tab and told me I'm supposed to put your chocolate milk and pie on there too, Tallie."

"Dang, if I'd known he was paying, I would have ordered one of everything." Marcy Graybill laughed and took the dishes away. "We don't want her talking, and laughter is a good distraction," I said to Max.

"I never question your methods."

"You might question this next move," I said as I scooted out of the booth with determination singing in my veins and curiosity burning up my brain.

"Where's Grams?"

"Sweetie, it's so nice to see you again. I thought you'd be sick of us by now." Mom stood in the doorway of their house, wrapped in her robe. It was late, and I knew I was coming around past *Jeopardy!* so I risked waking up everyone. But I needed to talk with Grams, and my mom, too.

"I love you, Mom, and I think it's going to be many years before I get sick of you." The thought of Burton and his father's relationship made me step forward and give her a big hug that she returned without a second's hesitation.

"Come on in. I'll go get her. I warn you, I think she has her face cream on, so don't say anything about the green."

"I learned my lesson about that when I was six." I'd asked her if she was an alien, and she'd yelled at me until I crumpled on the floor. Of course at that age, that was about two words' time, but still. I hadn't known any better, and she'd always scared me after that. But I needed

something now and she might have it. Time to wade in.
I'd survived dinner. I'd survive this too.

Mom left us in the kitchen, where I grabbed the snowman cookie jar from the top of the refrigerator. This
would require sugary reinforcement. If I'd had a latte, I'd
have been even happier, but I'd probably also still be up
four hours from now and it was already almost nine-
thirty.

I was going to have all kinds of holiday weight to get
rid of when the calendar flipped to January. I'd eaten
more in the last few days than I'd eaten in the last month
or so.

I heard Grams grumbling before I saw her and knew
that I might need to throw Max in front of me to defuse
her before I asked her anything.

"What is it that you want, young lady?" Sure enough,
her whole face was green and her hair was up in curlers. I
didn't know how she slept like that. I'd tried when I was
in elementary school and had the worst headache when I
woke up and decided curls would never be worth that
again.

"You know more than you said earlier about this
Hoagie thing."

She narrowed her eyes at me. "I told you everything I
know, and it's not much." Her eyes shifted to the left and
then the right.

"So you say, but I don't believe it."

My mom cleared her throat. "She just said she told you
everything, dear. It's late and you're being rude. What are
you getting at?"

"I listened to a podcast the other day about being able
to spot liars, and the shifty-eye thing is all too real. Grams

knows more than she's saying. I'm just here for her to tell me the rest, because I think it has a lot to do with what is going on."

Mom gasped. "You have got to be kidding me."

Grams grunted, then stuck her hands on her hips.

"No, I'm not. Eye rolling like she just did doesn't count, but looking to the left is a sure sign of lying. So cough it up, Grams." Apparently, I was going all out on throwing all caution to the wind. Maybe it wouldn't backfire on me, but I had a feeling I knew exactly what she was going to do.

And then she did. She snorted at me, turned on her heel and walked away.

"You know there's a woman dead and a man missing. If you have anything about why this might be happening and you don't share it, you could be considered an accessory to murder. Unless you're the one who hit her on the head?" I called after her.

Even though I was doing my own lying on that last part, it still got her to turn around.

She stomped back and clenched her hand in the robe fabric at her throat. "You go too far. I like Max, so I'm not going to say what's on my mind, but I'll have you know you are not going to threaten me."

She'd called my bluff, and I deflated. "I'm sorry." I rubbed my forehead. "I just want to find out what happened, and I feel like you know more than you've shared." I swallowed. "I don't want anyone else to die. What if whoever killed Ronda knows the secret and is going after anyone else who knows? What if you're next?" I dropped my head along with my gaze and looked at my shoes. I needed some new tennies. These were getting worn out and because I could afford them now, I should think about going shopping.

She scoffed. "Now you're trying to play my game of making people feel bad so they'll do whatever I want them to do."

I peeked up at her. "Is it working?"

Chapter Nineteen

She turned on her heel again and stalked off. I'd blown it. I'd tried my maximum sass factor and I'd lost, and now it was probably going to be even worse for my mother to deal with Grams for the next six days. Then again, maybe she'd leave early and decide not to ever come back.

I wanted to like her, I really did, but her attitude and her anger made it hard to do anything more than love her from afar. I had found out with her early on that you could love someone without actually liking them, or what they did to your family. It wasn't a lesson I'd have to share with Max because I knew he felt the same way about his grandmother. That saying about not being able to pick your family was incredibly true. Sure, Grams had unbent a little to like Max and tell my mom that she'd raised us right, but would it last?

"I'm sorry, Mom. She's probably going to take it out on you now."

"Pshh, don't worry about it. I've had worse. She'll get over it. Hey, if nothing else, you just gave yourself a pass to not spend any time with her over the next few days. I guess I'll count the two of you out for dinner tomorrow. You probably have enough leftovers to last you for the next few weeks anyway."

Now I felt horrible. I wasn't cut out for this kind of thing. I would never be the bad cop. Maybe I could effectively be the person who was in the wrong place at the right time, or the one people ignored and talked in front of about stuff they shouldn't, but confrontation was not my forte. I should have remembered that before I tried to go toe-to-toe with the dragon lady.

The dragon lady, who I could hear stomping back down the stairs. I grabbed Max's hand to leave before she made it into the kitchen, but I wasn't fast enough.

"Don't you move. You want to go at me, let's go. Set your fanny down at this table and be prepared for a story that might just blow your socks off."

"Can I have some tea with that?" I asked my mother.

She smiled and put a kettle on.

"Let's roll." I sat at the table across from my grand-mother and prepared to have my adorable lobster socks knocked right off.

She placed a Bible on the table between us. Max took a seat to my right and Mom wandered over to lean a hip against the counter to the left of Grams.

"About forty years ago, Hal Burton came to your grandfather. They were best friends. He had a favor to ask and knew that it could be a problem if it ever got out, so he took your grandfather into the library we'd had built onto the back of the house. They sat in there for over an hour, talking."

"Did you listen at the door?" I asked before I could stop myself.

She drew herself up tight and stared down her nose at me. "The best do. There's no need to be ignorant of a situation, and I knew your grandfather probably wouldn't tell me everything. He rarely did." She sniffed. "Now, are you going to interrupt me every few sentences, or do you want me to tell you what you so rudely demanded to know?"

I snapped my mouth shut on my next question and nodded at her.

"Good; at least you have enough sense to know when to stop. There might be hope for you yet. Especially with Max around." With that, she gave him an absolutely sweet smile, then turned to glare at me.

"Thank you, ma'am. I think." He grabbed my hand.

"And manners," she cooed.

I rolled my eyes and made the go-on motion with my free hand. "Absolutely awesome. Everyone loves Max, and he's the epitome of gentility. Who knows why he's with me in the first place with my near hopelessness? Can we get on with it?"

"Fine. I like that even better than manners." Grams flipped open the Bible in front of her, and the whole thing was hollow, like one of those safes that people in medieval times used to hide their most precious belongings. I'd seen her carry that thing all over the place, and here the whole time it hadn't held scripture but little pieces of paper I desperately wished I could take the time to see what she'd written on them.

For the moment, though, she took out one folded piece of paper and smoothed it out on the table in front of her.

"I want that Bible when you go." I kept my eye on it. Who knew what kind of secrets were in there?

"No, dear, your father already has very strict orders to burn the thing when I pass. It will be cremated with me."

"Can I just peek at it?"

"I don't think so. Now, back to the reason we're sitting here." She ran a hand over the paper again, then took the glasses that hung on the chain around her neck and perched them on her nose. "'One Maurice Howard and everyone he brings with him is to be kept in the strictest confidence as Hoagie Hogart and family. Introduce him to the family as such and in return, you and your family will be given a free pass on speeding tickets as long as they are under twenty miles over the limit, as well as access to the gentlemen's club on York, the American Legion on Main, and the Society of Mechanicsburg's finest for the length of your line. Thank you and my deepest regards. Signed, Hal Burton.'"

"Wait, no speeding tickets? As in no speeding tickets ever for everyone that comes from Granddad and you?" My eyes went wide.

"That's the one thing you pulled from all that?" Max said as Mom and Grams laughed.

"No, I got the other part, too, but this means Burton owes me money for all those tickets he's given me over the years for one-to-five miles over the speed limit. I am so going to hold him to this after I deal with the fact that it sounds like Hoagie was part of the witness protection program and might be in serious danger if someone in his past is coming after him and his family."

I had a lot to think about and a lot to do, but first I

glanced at the clock and saw that it was nearing ten. I'd had a full day, and Max along with me. He started work with my dad tomorrow. I should get him home to sleep before he messed up his first day with one of the most demanding bosses known to me.

The next day I had gone over the firebug info with Max a handful of times before he had to report downstairs for work and nothing more was coming to me. It looked like Sherman had done an incredibly thorough job. I wished I could give him something, but because I didn't have anything, I would just keep my mouth shut for the moment.

Plus, I had bigger things to go after, like all that money I'd given to the borough over the years for tickets, and I had to go talk to Burton's dad.

But first, I had lost track of the cleaning schedule and wasn't even sure what day it was, much less if I was set to clean anything today.

So I checked the schedule online for clients, and it looked like we had a big job over at the Clemenses', and were double-booked at the Stapletons'. I called Letty to see what had happened.

"Oh, thank you so much for seeing that. I was just about to check because I got those notifications you set up and was wondering what had happened. I can make it work, though. I'll just hand the big job to Annie, then ask if I can move the schedule back for the one extra. I'm sure it will be fine."

"Where's Jenna?"

"She said she can't come in and might actually be quitting, depending on what happens with Nathan."

"What? We're going to have to hire someone new ASAP then. Let me know if you know anyone. I'm a little peeved that she didn't talk to me, but I guess there's not much I can do about that now."

"Will do, boss lady."

"Okay, well the Stapletons aren't going to be happy about having to be moved back." I paused and flipped through my own calendar. As much as I liked the one on my phone, I still had to keep paper. I remembered things better if I wrote them down instead of typing them. Witness my own little folder of info at my elbow of all the things I'd found out so far. I still hadn't made any other connections and might have a clearer picture once I talked with Burton's father, but that wasn't scheduled until later this afternoon, around three. Right after bingo. Yes, bingo. I couldn't get away from it.

"I don't have anything at the moment, now that I know what day it is. Why don't you ask Camilla to help with the Stapletons and I'll come to the Clemenses' with you?"

"You're not supposed to be helping this week. Remember, you were taking a vacation? I'm supposed to be able to handle this all by myself."

"Seriously? You do so much, and unless you're offended that I'm trying to step on your toes, I'm helping. In fact, even if you are offended, you'll just have to get over it."

She laughed. "Hey, it's your company. I'm certainly not going to turn down help from the boss."

"And while we're there, I'd like to talk to you about the things we heard at Hoagie's daughter's house." That felt like a week ago but was mere days. "A couple of things have been bothering me, and I just haven't had time to get with you on them. This way we can get paid while we talk."

I could almost hear her shrug over the phone. "Whatever works for you. I want this person caught too, and anything I can do to help I'll do."

"See you in forty minutes, then."

We said our goodbyes and I checked in with Max to find him screwing some bookshelves into the wall.

"I thought you were going to work with my father this morning."

He looked up with a mask over his mouth and nose and his eyes crinkled. "I can do this." The words were muffled, but I'd heard them often enough that I knew exactly what he was saying.

"Whatever floats your boat, but I thought maybe we could go out to lunch today if you're free from training with my father and because you're no longer going to be looking for tax clients."

He shrugged and took off the mask. "Are you sure you're okay with this? I offered without talking to you, but I saw a way to help out you and your family and took it instead of thinking it all the way through."

"Are you having second thoughts? Because no one will blame you if you are."

"No. Actually, I'm not having second thoughts at all. I think it will be interesting to try this out and see what it entails. And then I was thinking I might go back to school to get the degrees I need if I like it enough."

Wow, that was a step or seven beyond just helping out with the family business, but he looked like he meant it. And after everything he had done to support me in whatever my current career choice was, I certainly wasn't going to keep him from pursuing whatever he wanted to do.

"The training is extensive. I'm not saying that to put you off; I just don't know how much of your current schooling will count toward what you want to do. There's a lot of anatomy stuff if you want to be able to prepare the bodies." I knew, because I had looked into all the classes and had used my complete lack of wanting to manhandle dead people as a reason for not pursuing it in college.

Funny that I still seemed to deal with the dead, even if I didn't have to actually touch them beyond checking that they in fact really had no pulse.

"We'll cross that bridge when we get there. For now, I can help with a lot of the business stuff and am going to look over the business taxes to see if there's anything I can do, or any suggestions I can make to save some money on what your dad pays out every year."

"I'm sure he'll love that."

"And I'm making your mom cash your checks for rent."

I laughed long and loud. "How'd you get her to do that?"

"I told your father she hadn't been doing it, and that any checks they wouldn't honor because they were out-dated would be replaced immediately by me. And because I can't stand my accounts being out of order, they'd have to take them to the bank immediately or I'd hand them cash."

I laughed some more and kissed him on the cheek. "You know, the day you snuck into town and pretended to be a flower delivery guy is ranked as one of the best days of my life—even if I did try to have you arrested for leaving flowers on our doorstep."

"Every day since then has been a good one." He smiled back at me with dust in his hair and a mask hanging around his strong neck.

"Even the one when you got nailed in the face with a vase of flowers?"

"Even that one." He hugged me tight and then got back to work.

I had to get to work myself, so I ran for a quick shower to wash off the dust he'd just transferred to me and then dressed for more dust and dirt. The Clemenses weren't unsanitary people; they just weren't much for picking up after themselves. When I'd written their contract and priced their house, I had been careful to take into account how much I'd have to do. And now that Letty primarily handled their house, I was very thankful I had.

She was faster than I was, but it still took time. And she deserved to be paid for that.

Heading over to Coover Street, I took in the way the town was still festooned with lights. Most people kept them up until at least New Year's Day, after the wrench dropped from the fire truck on Main Street at midnight. Then we'd take down the decorations and eat pork and sauerkraut on the first day of the year for good luck.

Trees were naked of their leaves but decked out in lights for all the world to see. The smell of snow on the breeze came in my window, and so did a whiff of . . . smoke?

As if in answer to my question, the fire alarms in town—all three of them—started blaring. Within seconds, the trucks were running, with sirens lit up and letting any traffic know they were coming through.

Could this be a Sherman firebug fire? I quickly turned onto the street before any trucks could come up behind me. The streets were narrow in this section of town, and with so many people parking in front of their houses instead of at the back of their long but narrow properties, it could be hard to pull over to let the trucks pass. As soon as I made the right, though, I knew I wasn't going to be cleaning today, at least not in the way I normally did.

The Clemens house was the one on fire, and Letty's car was there, but I didn't see her on the sidewalk or in the driver's seat.

Chapter Twenty

I parked my car and jumped out. Spotting a passerby, I called out to the kid walking down the street with his earbuds in to get him to call 911, but he must not have heard me. Dang technology! I was of course smart enough not to go into a burning house for my friend, but the temptation was overwhelming to do just that. I had made it to the sidewalk and was about to ignore my better instincts when the first fire truck pulled up.

Sherman was out in full gear and shoved me back.

"I think Letty might be in there," I yelled, in case he couldn't hear me through his helmet and whatever else they wore on their heads to protect themselves. He gave me a thumbs-up and then must have communicated that to his guys because they picked up their pace and took down the door in one move.

I moved back out of their and harm's way, knowing

that they'd do their job and do it well. And would save my friend in the process.

What followed was the longest three minutes of my life. Hoses were run and hooked up, men ran back and forth to make sure everything was in place and then water shot from the hoses like a typhoon.

And a man emerged carrying out my friend and employee in his arms. I had never in my life felt such relief and anger at the same time.

Sherman pushed me back when I automatically went for her. My anger rose to overshadow my relief, but then I saw how dirty everyone was and tamped down my first reaction to wait for what happened next. At least she was breathing and coughing, and she looked pissed enough to take on the world all by herself.

That was my girl.

I used the time while the EMTs checked her out to text Max to make sure he knew where I was and that I was okay. I also asked him to start looking harder at that firebug file. If this was the same person, we had moved to a new level and things had just gotten very personal. I wanted to find out who had killed Ronda. I really did, but this had just moved up to the top of the list of things I wanted taken care of. After I talked to Burton's dad, I would leave the rest to Burton. Maybe this once I needed to step out and do what I could where I was needed most.

Ray, the EMT who constantly harassed me every time we met, had no laughs today. He did beckon me over once he'd checked Letty over.

"Some smoke inhalation and a definite scare, but we got her out in time. She'll be at the hospital being processed if you want to follow behind."

Letty sat huddled in a blanket with tears running through the soot on her face.

"Do you have clean underwear on?' I asked her. "Your mom's gone, so someone has to ask before they take you to the hospital."

That got a smile and a laugh. "My God, how scary was that? It was like the whole place went up in flames after that little jerk ran away."

"Wait, little jerk? Who did you see?"

"I have no idea. All I know is he had dark hair and was about six feet tall."

Which made him not so little compared to my just-five-foot-tall friend. But I was thinking it meant that her impression of him had been that he was younger. I could work with that, because dark hair and male described about a quarter of the people in town. Young meant it cut that number in about half.

"Let these guys take care of you. I'll find out what happened from Sherman."

"You'd better get him, Tallie. He set the thing on fire with a lit piece of paper in a can and then ran down the street toward the church on Frederick."

The fact that she remembered that impressed me immensely. Always on the lookout, that was my Letty, and I had never been so thankful that someone was paying attention.

"I'll let Sherman know. Good powers of observation."

"Not that it got me out of the house in time, because I was already upstairs when the flames started licking at the floor, but it's something."

"Why don't I follow you to the hospital, make sure you get settled in and then I'll come back and talk to Sherman?"

"No, I can take care of myself. Just text Jenna to see if she wouldn't mind bringing me some new clothes. She's at the Stapletons' but at this point they can wait for all I care. I want clean clothes. And then, when you're done, you can come by if you want."

Expecting someone else to take care of her while I stayed to talk to Sherman didn't sit very well with me, but I understood where she was coming from.

Once the ambulance drove away, I looked around. I'd promised Letty I would be there soon, but she'd told me again to do this instead of following her around because she could take care of herself. I found Sherman standing next to the new fire truck with his gloves tucked under his arm.

"Letty says she saw a guy running away from the house when she was upstairs and he used a lit piece of paper in a can to ignite the fire. He ran off toward the church on Frederick."

I gave him the details she'd given me as best I could. Sherman's eyes went wide and he barked out orders like an army sergeant. I waited, not wanting to interfere if it meant we could catch this guy right now instead of later.

"Already helping, I see." He smiled at me, even though he looked incredibly weary.

"Trying, anyway."

"No, it's more than we had before, so I appreciate it. I just wish I could figure out what he was using so we could get a lead on where he's getting it."

I looked around for any clues without leaving my spot by his side. The fire still was not contained, though they were working diligently on it. I'd never been this close to a scene like this, and part of me was fascinated by the way the flames jumped and danced behind the curtains before consuming them. The other part of me was seriously proud of our men in town who went in and out without hesitation to save not only the structure but also themselves.

"I want this guy, Tallie, and I want him now. He went too far this time."

"Do you think he believed the house was empty? The Clemenses always leave for us to clean. Maybe he knew that, or watched them all pile into their car, and decided to go for it, not knowing that Letty was coming in?"

"It's possible and would stick with what he's done before. But is he watching certain streets waiting for people to leave? Does he already have a house picked out or just a street? I can't seem to get anything to make sense right now and it's irritating me, not to mention making me angry and look bad in town. We have to get this sorted out."

I patted his big, rough jacket. "We will. We can't do anything at this point, so I'm going to go home and go through that paperwork you gave me with a fine-tooth comb. I promise."

"You come up with anything, you let me know immediately."

"Of course, Uncle Sherman."

And with that, I took myself to my car and went home.

Well, at least I'd helped a little, though I was sure Sherman would have gotten the same information when he talked with Letty after her stay in the hospital.

Arriving back at home, I knocked on the wall to let Max know I was here. He was so engrossed in the stack of paper in front of him on the kitchen table that he just waved a hand at me.

It was nearing lunchtime, so I went about putting together some leftovers from my mom's house and microwaving them. Fuel for the brain was going to be necessary if I hoped to find anything to help Sherman.

What was going on in our town? First murderers started cropping up a little over a year ago, and now an arsonist.

Well, we'd have one down before too long because I wasn't going to sit on my rear end waiting to see what happened next. Proactive was about to become my new middle name. Forget Tenacity *and* Beverly.

Max and I must have sat for three hours poring over things. Letty had called to tell me that they were releasing her from the hospital, so there was no need for me to come down to sit with her before she left.

She called me again when she got home and said she was going to take a nap. I asked if she wanted me to bring her car around, but she said she'd pick it up later.

Still, I wanted to go check things out again. Maybe there was something there the guys had missed. No matter what, I wanted at that house. It might not be a dead body, and I might not have to catch a murderer, but this was still superimportant.

Whether he'd meant to or not, he'd hurt my friend, and that just was not acceptable in my book.

Taking Max with me this time, we went back to Coover Street. The whole house was intact as far as I could see. The outside looked like it had every other day I'd I driven by it.

But there was a faint tang of smoke still hanging in the air. At least the fire hadn't jumped to any other houses. That was a constant concern with how close things were built around here. The side of your house was the beginning of the next person's yard, with only about ten feet of grass or open space. We had tons of row homes too, and those were even more concerning.

That wasn't my problem at the moment, though. The house in front of me was.

"Do you see anything out of the norm?" I asked Max.

"Other than the fact that inside is as black as night, I'm not really sure what I'd be looking for, Tallie. Is that swing set usually there? Shouldn't they have shoveled their sidewalk by now? Toys on the front lawn are normal for someone who has kids, I would think. But what about that kitschy water fountain and the wishing well? Isn't it normal to shut those things down during winter in case the pipes freeze?"

"You're not helping."

Max shrugged. "This is all very new to me."

"Me too. I have no idea what I'm doing here, and Sherman keeps asking me to find something, anything, to help him and I don't know what to do."

"It's okay not to fill in all the gaps for everyone."

"But he was so nice with his compliments and his ego stroking, while Burton used to yell at me. Sherman is actually asking me to help and I feel like I should be able to just hand him the arsonist on a silver platter."

Max took my hand in his and kissed my knuckles. "This is what happens when you show people how smart you are."

I laughed. "Not necessarily Einstein, but I'm not an idiot either, and I feel like there's something here we should see."

"Same thing with all the paperwork. But that's not how you do things. Why don't you see if you can get in to clean this house like Sherman asked you to? Maybe whatever it is you're supposed to see is actually inside."

"And what might I ask are *you* doing here?" With that kind of phrasing, that really could have been anyone behind me because I always seemed to be where I wasn't supposed to be.

I turned to find Bertie Myers and his crew crossing the street from their van. I'd been so deep in concentration that I hadn't heard a car on the street at all, much less his big, old van, which had seen better days. For all the cleanup he'd been doing lately, I seriously hoped he might invest in a higher-quality vehicle, then maybe get a professional to stencil the side of it instead of using a permanent marker and some stencils he'd made with paper bags.

"Bertie, how's it going? Sherman just asked me to come over to look at the house to see what it might need."

"Oh, bless you. Does that mean we might have help? I swear, with this person running around I'm about tuckered out. I've never been this busy before. I have dishpan hands from cleaning stuff even wearing my rubber gloves."

Did he really mean that or was he just playing me? I rarely had anyone so happy to see me, and I would technically be taking away some of his business. I was going to assume he really was happy for the help and not second guess him or myself.

"Bertie, if you really want help, I can get a few of my people on site for you."

"Oh dear, would you do that? I would be so thankful. I don't know what else to do and I want to get these people back into their houses and back to normal life. The money's good of course, but I feel horrible putting people off because we have too many sites to clean." Bertie wiped his brow with a rag, even though it was barely above freezing out here. Did men go through hot flashes?

The rest of his crew had shown up on the sidewalk and were milling around. I caught one of them giving me an angry look; then he looked away when I stared him down.

"I'm happy to help, but it looks like some of your people might not like that idea."

Bertie looked around and zeroed in on the tall guy with the light hair standing off to the side, the one who'd glared at me.

"We're all fine with this and know it's important to have the people back in their homes, more important than collecting big money. We'd be happy to split the charge with you if you don't mind bringing your own chemicals." He looked in the front windows of the house behind me. "This is going to be a big job, but I have to finish the Franklins' house before I can get here."

Zeke, Bertie's son, put a hand on his father's shoulder. "We've got this, old man. I swear we'll be able to get it all done, and then we can take a break for a little while hopefully. The season of irresponsible people with flammable trees is almost over, and then it might be a grease fire or two for a little if we're lucky." Where Bertie's hair was white and poofed out around his ears, leaving the top of his head bald, Zeke had a full head of light brown hair. I looked a little more closely at him. Letty wasn't old by any means—in fact, she and Zeke were probably about the same age—but Zeke had a very youthful face. And if he'd been hit by soot from the fire or smoke, his hair might have been darker, or maybe it had seemed darker when seen through the smoke Letty had been trying to escape.

Could he be the one who was setting the fires? Not only did it bring in money, but he'd know the mechanics of a fire and all the things that could be done to set them off. Had I called out to him to call 911 when I'd arrived at the fire and he'd ignored me because he'd set it? I'd thought he was a kid at the time, but I could have been wrong. Then again, I thought anyone under thirty was a kid, so there was that.

I filed the information back in my brain as I smiled and worked out the details with Bertie. Once things were settled, I turned to Max.

"Are you working today?"

"In an hour or so your dad wants me to come into the basement to work with Clarissa, who does hair for the funerals."

I shuddered. That was one of my least favorite things to be a part of. Especially if the person had broken their neck or had head trauma. Clarissa was a magician, though, not just a beautician, and did an amazing job even with the hardest cases.

"Okay, well then, why don't you go do that and I'll get the crew together to sort out who can do what?"

"Whatever works for you. I could probably help with the cleaning too, if you want. I'll just be a Max-of-all-trades."

I snickered. "I might just take you up on that while Letty's recovering. I don't know when she'll be back on her feet."

Bertie was talking to his three employees and pointing things out when I looked back at him. "I want to help, but I don't want to spread everyone too thin."

"We can get it all done. No fear," Max said

"Yeah," I said as I watched him walk away and turn the corner to go back to the funeral home.

"You know, if you don't have time, we really can handle this ourselves." Zeke was back at my side while everyone else was grabbing tools from Bertie's van.

"If your dad wants my help, I'd like to offer it." I eyed him up and down. He was tall, and if Letty had thought he was younger than he really was, it was very possible I was staring at the firebug. "It's weird how many fires have happened over the last few weeks. It's almost like they're deliberate."

He flinched and pulled at the collar of his shirt, then yanked his hand back down to his side. "I highly doubt that. Who would do something like that? We're a good town."

"Even good towns have people who do bad things. I heard that there might have been some accelerant used. Something that's hard to come by. The fire chief was looking into where it might be available and how you'd go about buying it last I heard." A total lie, because my uncle had no idea, but why not put that out there and see what happened?

Zeke just scoffed. "He's looking for something that doesn't exist."

Bertie called over for Zeke and he waved to his dad.

"You'd better get going." I waited to see if he'd say anything more. He opened his mouth and closed it, then opened it again.

"Don't go looking for trouble where there is none. Don't you have your hands full enough with trying to do Burton's job and now trying to horn in on my dad's cleanup business? I'd think you would want to just stick with your little cleaning crew. Don't get mixed up with the big boys."

Well, that sounded a little like a threat and too tempting to pass up. "Zeke, you have no idea who you're talking to if you think I can't take on and demolish the big boys. I've had a lot of practice."

"Zeke, now! I need you over here to make sure we're all on the same page with this cleanup, boy." Bertie stood with a clipboard in one hand and the other on his waist.

"Better scoot along, *boy*." If pressed, I would admit that calling him "boy" was above and beyond what I should have said, but I was irritated with how much was going on around my small town and didn't need to be told where my place was.

My place was wherever I wanted it to be. And if someone asked for my help, I was going to do my best to help in an effort to continue to atone for abandoning everyone in this town when I was too stuck up to realize how I'd shunned the very people who'd meant so much to me. Bertie was another one. He'd let me work with him when I was eighteen before I went off to college. I vaguely knew what I was doing regarding fire cleanup, and Zeke could just go stuff it.

To prove my point, I took out my phone and started taking pictures of the house while they stood out on the sidewalk talking. I got shots through the window as best I could.

I was about to walk away when I realized there was something strange inside the house on the foyer floor that hadn't been touched by the fire. A wig; a dark wig.

Digging the key out of the flowerbed, I opened the back door and snuck in, trying to keep low in case anyone on the sidewalk looked in the window while I was being stealthy.

With my phone, I took a picture of it where it lay on the floor, then ran to the kitchen to get a paper towel to pick it up and a plastic bag from the pantry to put it in. Sherman was going to have to ask the Clemenses if either of them wore a wig or one of their kids cosplayed, but I had a feeling this didn't belong to them. It smelled like fire, but with a strong undertone of man sweat.

I had just tucked the bag into my jacket against my belly when the front door opened. Bertie made a sound of surprise, but I got a beady-eyed glare from Zeke.

"It looks like it's going to need a lot of work in here," I said with sunshine in my voice. "I'll call you later, Bertie, to set up a schedule. I'm sure the girls will be more than happy to help."

I waved on my way out and ignored the under-the-breath snarl from Zeke. He might talk a big game, but I could go one better. I did every time. Ask Burton.

Chapter Twenty-one

After dropping off the wig to a jubilant Sherman and telling him my theory, I headed over to the old folks' home on Keller. I was going to be a couple of minutes late, but hopefully Hal Burton wouldn't notice.

I should not have thought that, or even hoped for it, knowing what his kid was like. Burton had to come by his attitude somehow, and I knew his mother had been a sweetheart.

"You ask for a meeting and then you aren't on time. That's no way to treat anyone, much less an old man who has things to do." The old man in question thumped his cane on the floor hard enough to make the guy next to him jump and topple over from his low chair.

I beat the male orderly, who smelled of man sweat and smoke, as I rushed to grab his arm to make sure he didn't hit the floor and realized it was another uncle of mine.

Actually great-uncle, or maybe great-great-uncle, perhaps a cousin four times removed. I'd have to ask my dad when I talked to him next.

"I've got him, thanks," I said to the kid, the same one I'd seen on Bertie's crew. "You work here too?"

"I do a lot of things, but I'm off shift now, so make sure he doesn't fall again." He frowned at me as if I had been the one to push the old guy off the chair.

Ignoring him, I turned back to the frail senior. "You okay, Mr. Brannigan?"

"Barbara? Barbara, is that you? Did you bring me cookies, girl? They never let me have any sweets here, and you know how much I love my sweets. Tell me you brought me cookies," he pleaded while clawing at my arm.

Glancing over his head, I caught the eye of a nurse and nodded her over. She hustled over and helped me with the grasping man.

"I'll make sure to bring some next time, Mr. Brannigan. Promise."

"You'd better. They're going to be your entrance fee. No cookies, no time with your favorite uncle, girl. And it's Uncle Bruce, not Mr. Brannigan. I've told you that before."

Seriously, I didn't know what to say to that, and this was one time when I really didn't want to lie because I wasn't sure which Barbara he was referring to.

I looked over at the nurse and she winked at me as she took him by his elbow. "I'll handle it. I can offer him something he hates, then make it sweet by giving him what he'd prefer," she murmured to me. Then she raised her voice. "It's time for your tapioca pudding, Mr. Brannigan; that will be nice and sweet. You love your tapioca pudding."

"Ha! I want a cookie, not pudding. Tapioca looks like it has maggots in it. Can I at least have chocolate this time?"

"Of course." The nurse looked back at me again and winked.

"He falls for it every single damn time." Hal Burton snorted in disgust. "I'll never be that stupid."

"Are you a fan of tapioca pudding?"

"Hate the stuff." He glared at me.

"And so, if they offered you chocolate, you'd turn that down." I waited to be seated until he offered. We'd already gotten off to a bad start, but I had a feeling this was going to be like Zeke; you had to show no fear and let them know you weren't going to take their flack or you'd get stepped all over.

"Of course not. I already told you I would never be that stupid."

"Good to know." I opened my purse and handed him a plastic baggie of cookies. "I'm told they're oatmeal, which I know isn't quite as sweet as pudding." Burton had also told me that they were his absolute favorite. I hadn't had time to whip them up myself, so I'd bought them at the grocery store, but he probably wouldn't know the difference. Although, on second thought, I could be playing with fire here if he was offended.

He took a bite of the first cookie, then harrumphed. "Store-bought. Next time bring me the real thing."

"Sure." I reached out to take back the bag and he snatched it out of my grasp, then clutched it to his bony chest.

"Don't even try. I might be old, but I'm still quick on the draw."

"I'm told no one is really old until they're a hundred and seven." I figured he wasn't actually going to offer me a seat, so I took one. My legs were tired from running around over the last few days, and he was just going to have to live with me not waiting for his invitation, just like he would have to be fine with the store-bought cookies.

He took another bite and sighed. That was a sigh of satisfaction, and it made me wish I had taken the time to bake the cookies. He would have done more than sigh for those.

"If you ask my son, I was old before I even retired." He took another bite and yanked the hunk off with his dentures. They were way too straight and white to be his real teeth.

"Ah, Burton, my nemesis." If he despised his son as much as Burton thought he did, would playing Hal's ally work in my favor?

"Nemesis, ha! I heard you're trying to replace him, not take him down."

Oh, that could be dangerous territory. "I'm not trying to replace him. I'm just helping him."

"Yeah, help him lose his job. Back in my day, we never would have let a common citizen solve our cases for us. We didn't involve them at all. We took care of things and no one was the wiser exactly what was going on in their little town. All the secrets, the lies, and the people who weren't as good as they said they were."

"But not the ones who weren't who they said they were?" I slipped in the question, interrupting his tirade and making him shove the rest of the cookie into his mouth. I sat while he chewed and then swallowed. He picked another cookie and bit into that one too, staring at me the whole time. I smiled to let him know I was happy he was enjoying the cookie. "I'm not going anywhere until I get some answers, so you just enjoy that cookie and talk whenever you're ready. Unless you want me to call the nurse back over? She might take your cookies, but there's tapioca pudding on the menu."

"You're underhanded."

"I get the job done." I shrugged.

"You're undermining my son," he fired back.

"I'm helping him close cases before they get out of hand or before they go cold. I don't try to get involved unless it means something to me, and these have meant something to me. Plus, people tell me things that maybe they shouldn't. Like my grandmother . . ." I left that hanging there for a moment while he took the last cookie out of the baggie.

"I wondered why you were coming by when I've never had you visit before. I thought maybe it was just to gloat, or because Shirley had guilted you in to doing community service for all that time you thought we were beneath you."

Oh, a jab, and one that would have hurt far more a few months ago. Now, I just smiled at him. "That was the old me. I'm all about helping now and have made peace with everyone. Cookies seem to go a long way to get people talking."

"We're having a parallel conversation. Well done."

"Thanks."

"That's it, just thanks?" He shoved the last piece of oatmeal cookie in his mouth, then looked sadly at the empty baggie.

I took the second baggie out of my purse and put it on my lap.

"Well, damn, girl."

At that, I laughed. "I gave you something you wanted and then I held back the rest in case you wouldn't cooperate."

"Is that what you do with my kid?"

I scoffed. "No, I try my hardest to help your son, and he's about as stubborn as you are. The apple didn't even roll slightly from the tree as far as I can see."

"Nothing wrong with that."

"Not at all. Except when it comes to getting either of you to tell me what I need to know to get things moving in the right direction."

He eyed the bag of cookies and then used the back of his hand to wipe at the corner of his mouth. I fought with myself not to just hand them to him. But they were my bargaining tool, and I couldn't give in without getting some answers.

"So, tell me about Hoagie and I'll give you the cookies plus the third bag I was going to give the staff when I left."

"They don't need the cookies. They can go home and gorge on them anytime they want."

"And I can go home with this last bag and eat them myself . . . or I can open them right now and enjoy them."

"Fine, fine, fine. You got me. Give me the cookies and I'll tell you a story."

"Tell me a story and I'll judiciously hand out the cookies at specific intervals."

He laughed, and I knew I was in. Now to find out what had really happened, what kind of person I was actually looking for and whether I really wanted to find Hoagie.

I settled into the surprisingly comfy visitor's chair and tried to block out the smell of antiseptic sitting just under the scent of deodorizer. It wasn't a lot different from the smell in the basement of the funeral home. I certainly wasn't going to say that out loud, but it stayed in the back of my head as I waited for Hal Burton to start.

"I wasn't told very much when the marshal came to me and asked me to take Hoagie on. We didn't have computers and that type of thing back then, so I just had to trust that the witness to a crime they were sending me was going to keep himself out of further trouble and not really discuss what he'd seen in the first place. I knew it had to do with his brother, though. He was going to be in hiding from him and his friends for years while his brother served a jail sentence."

"Did they tell you how long the sentence was?"

"Forty years. I've watched over him all these years, though. I'd considered taking him into our family instead of asking your grandfather, but with Shirley and her insatiable curiosity, it never would have flown. She would have grilled that poor man like she used to grill hot dogs for our family picnics."

I snickered, because Mama Shirley liked her dogs well done, like crispy black on the outside well done.

"You've had one of her dogs, then? The woman can cook the most elaborate things, but you give her a poor, defenseless piece of pseudo-meat that costs about three dollars a pound and she ruins it."

"I will not confirm or deny that because I can't have you using it against me at a later date."

He sighed. "I probably won't see you again once you get all your answers anyway, so what does it matter?"

Now I got a pang in my heart. Did anyone come to see

him? Burton didn't that I knew of. But maybe other people did? I could probably swing a visit every once in a while. I wouldn't offer now, but it was something I put in the back of my brain, along with the wig and Zeke's pissing match with the cleanup of the fires. There was a lot back there right now, but I'd just have to trust that it was all going to sort itself out right when I needed it.

"I'd come see you again and I can bring real cookies next time."

"Does your mom still make those snicker-doodles?"

"Yes, but my boyfriend tends to eat them all."

"Well, make him stop, or grab some before he gets to them. Those are my second favorite, right after oatmeal. I asked your dad to put some in my coffin with me when I'm gone, just in case I need something to hold me over while I hang around the gates of heaven until my slate is wiped clean."

I snorted. "Really? I hadn't heard about that."

"Well. I suppose I didn't ask your dad; I asked your grandfather. He said he put it in the paperwork. I believed him, but you might want to check when you go back to make sure it's still in there."

"I can do that as soon as you tell me what I want to know."

He sighed. "I got a call in the middle of the night that a guy and his family would be coming in the next day and buying Maynard Wright's store from him to sell the hardware. No one was to know who this guy was and we were all supposed to treat him like he'd been here forever. They were going to set him up with a new name and a new identity."

"Wait, are you saying he was officially part of the witness protection program? I thought he was just running from someone and you'd done a favor for a neighboring police station or something."

"No, nothing that small. Hoagie had turned in his twin brother for running with the wrong crowd and for setting up racketeering and gambling, loan sharking, I believe a murder or two. His twin brother got forty years in federal prison, but Hoagie's family was being threatened, so the government stepped in and hid him permanently by putting him in the program and starting him with a new life for his testimony."

Holy cow!

I handed over the last bag of cookies, said a quick thank-you and goodbye, then ran out of the retirement home. I had things to look in to and people to hunt down. Namely, one Maurice Howard aka Hoagie Hogart, who had seen more than he should and had hidden for forty years from his twin brother, Jerry Howard. How did I think I was going to be able to find someone who'd hidden for that long?

Hoagie had had years to be good at it, but maybe I could be better.

Chapter Twenty-two

I drove past the Clemens house on my way back home. I hoped Sherman would be able to figure something out from the wig I'd handed him. A break in one of the two cases going on would be something at least.

This information from Hal Burton was good too, though, and gave me a jumping-off point to see what Maurice Howard aka Hoagie Hogart had been up to before he'd moved to our town and pretended to be in our family for years.

Pulling in back of the funeral home, I got out of my car and made a beeline to the back door. I had a lot of things to do and not a lot of time to do them in if I wanted to keep anyone else from dying or going up in flames.

I must have been too loud with slamming the door behind me because my mom caught me at the bottom of the stairs.

"Tallie, if you have a moment?"

I really didn't, but I knew that with her mother here she might need to talk. I couldn't put her off forever.

"What's up, Mom?" I took my foot off the first stair while looking longingly up the flight to where my computer sat just waiting for me to search like I'd never searched before.

"I looked for more information on Hoagie and his family but wasn't able to find anything. I was wondering if maybe you thought you should follow up with Carl? He and Caitlin might have been old enough to remember life before they came here."

"Oh, that is a good idea." I leaned back against the oak banister with my arms and ankles crossed.

"Thanks. I do have one every now and again."

"You have them far more often than every now and again." I sat on the carpeted step. "Did you ever get to do what you wanted to do most, Mom? Was there a passion you had that you laid aside so Dad could pursue his dreams of playing with the dead?"

She waved a hand at me. "Oh, you. Your dad doesn't play with the dead, Tallie, and you know it. He serves an incredibly important purpose around here and I love helping him." She took a seat next to me on the stairs.

"But you didn't answer my question. Is there anything you really wanted to do that you didn't get to do?"

Leaning her head against the wallpaper, she looked at me. "I loved to paint when I was younger and thought I might do that someday. But it just never happened. Probably was a good thing too, because for some reason the paint thinner smelled like old broom closets mixed with incense. Plus, I did love to burn candles when I was younger and never paid attention to what they might be near. Did I ever tell you about the time I set one of my best dresses on fire? I was twirling around with this petticoat my mother had finally caved and gotten me and I tripped over the fashion magazine on the floor. Set myself on fire. I wouldn't have made it if it weren't for my mother thinking fast and throwing me to the ground so she could stomp on the dress."

"So, she is good sometimes?"

Mom laughed. "She's actually good a lot of the time. I know you see more of us fighting than not, and you probably think I'm weak for not standing up to her more often, but honestly, so many of the things she gets in a snit over just aren't worth it to me to fight about." She took my hand. "You kids, though? You were always worth fighting for. There were several things she wanted me to do in raising you that I absolutely refused to do. And look, she said you turned out okay after all."

Now it was my turn to laugh. "You have one son who likes to play in the dirt and is a big, old flirt, another who finally got his head out of the dead body business long enough to propose to the girl he was trying to convince they should get married to save his reputation and a daughter who is a mess."

"I'll give you the first two, but that last one is entirely untrue. I have a wonderful daughter who sees a need and tries to fill it no matter how it might affect her."

"And gets in trouble in the process."

"Well, there is that. But I wouldn't change a thing about you. I'm so happy you're back with us that I'd take you any way I could get you."

"Thanks."

"No, I mean it. If you never wanted to work another day here, I'd go up against your father to make sure he left you alone. I haven't done that yet because there are aspects that you seem to enjoy."

"I do like driving the hearse."

She chuckled and squeezed my hand. "I don't know how you park that thing. But that's beside the point. I raised a strong, independent daughter who knows her mind and that's never a bad thing. And you're helping both Burton and Sherman with things they can't figure out for themselves. You remind me of that lady on TV who wrote books and solved crimes."

"Jessica Fletcher?"

"That's the one. And I know you'll figure this all out too. If you need help, just give me a holler."

"I'm going to need some more snickerdoodles that you can't let Max have a crack at first. Hal Burton wants some for helping me."

"And did he help you?"

"Absolutely." A light went off in my head. "Actually, I think he helped me more than I realized." My leg started bouncing. "Mom, I have to go. I think I might have figured something out."

"Of course, dear. I'll bring those cookies up when they're ready."

"No rush on them. You can leave them in the kitchen when they're done. I'll grab them on my way out. Love you, Mom." I gave her a quick kiss and then ran up the stairs so fast I tripped on a few of them.

That click in my brain was way too big to ignore and I knew exactly what I was going to research and exactly how I was going to research it.

Fortunately, when I got into the apartment, it was empty except for the dog and cat. I filled both of their food bowls while I worked out exactly what I was going to look for.

And then I sat down and got to work.

Fifteen minutes later, I wanted to crow from a rooftop. It was all here, all of it, once I'd typed in the right words.

I knew from Grams that Maurice Howard was also Hoagie Hogart, but I hadn't put that together with the corpse in the basement. Maurice Howard was Jerry Howard's twin and had been on the run from the guy who'd died shortly after getting out of jail.

Online, there were a few grainy pictures of the trial, but it was enough to absolutely convince me that Hoagie and Maurice were definitely one and the same, and Jerry Howard must have been who he was running from.

It didn't tell me where he was now, but a theory was careening around inside my brain.

What if Hoagie had found out his brother was dead and killed Ronda to get to start over with a whole new life? He could leave the store to Nathan, allowing everyone to think he was dead, and then start over again somewhere else.

Not all the pieces fit into that scenario, but my concern at this point was that he might have skipped town and we'd never see him again.

I put in a quick call to the retirement home and got Hal Burton on the phone.

"This requires more cookies. I hate talking on the phone."

"I already asked my mom to make them and she's going to let me know when they're done. I'll bring them right over, but I think I might have figured something out and I need to confirm it with you."

"Shoot."

"Why a hardware store? Why did Hoagie get a hardware store when he started his new life?"

"He said it would be the perfect place to hide and make a new life for himself. He'd always liked building things, I guess, and thought that he might excel there. Why?"

"And when he moved here, did he have anything with him, like previous identification? Anything from his past?"

"I wouldn't know about that, but he was very interested in the safe in the floor that the hardware store had."

"Do you think he would have stored his stuff there?" I was thinking it had to be somewhere. From the articles I'd read about the trial, Hoagie had been very close with his family. Well, everyone except his brother. So, to have to leave and with how sentimental he was and what a good man he actually was, I couldn't imagine he had left with nothing.

"I would think the marshals would have confiscated all of that when they made a new life for him," he answered.

"But not necessarily."

"No, not necessarily," he agreed reluctantly.

"I'm going to go look."

He cleared his throat. "Tallie, I'm not going to tell you that you can't. I'm not even going to tell you it's a bad idea. But I am going to caution you and suggest that maybe you should just take this to my son and let him do his job."

"The one you don't think he's good enough at?"

He cleared his throat again. "I never said that. He's a

good cop, and I was happy to leave the department in his hands. I'm mad at him for leaving me in this old folks' home, but that doesn't mean I think he's no good at what he does."

An idea formed, but it would have to wait for a later time. "Okay, thanks for the help. I'll get those cookies to you as soon as I can. I appreciate everything you've given me."

"You'd better, and for all this I want a double batch. I'll hide them under the floorboards if I have to."

I chuckled as I disconnected. Under the floorboards. And that was probably doable with how old that place was. The hardware store wasn't exactly new either, and though the first floor had been turned to concrete some years ago, the upstairs was still wooden flooring, from what I remembered. Could that have been where the safe was?

Perhaps Nathan would know.

I figured at this point the hardware store should have reopened, and I wanted to get in there before it was sold off, either to Nathan or to a big corporation, depending on the true will.

Plus, I had to find Hoagie, and what better place to start looking than in his effects? Maybe now that his brother was dead, he'd go back to the place he started. It was at least worth a shot.

I was heading out the door when Max came in.

"Phew, that is going to take some getting used to." He plopped down on the couch and rested his head back against the top.

This deserved my attention more than anything else at the moment, though.

"Hard day at work, dear?"

He chuckled. "No, just weird and unusual and very informative. Did you know Clarissa can trowel on a layer of makeup over an inch think and it still looks natural? I didn't think that was possible. And she uses like forty-two different kinds of powders to bring the color back to the absolute white of the skin?"

I sat next to him with my hand on his knee. "I did. I've watched her perform her magic before. It is fascinating, even if it's weird."

"Fascinating. That's a good word. This is all fascinating. Your dad was trying to give me a tour, but I just couldn't stop going back to watch the transformation of Wilma Freedman from the Women's Auxiliary."

"There's nothing wrong with that." And I was going to have to truly accept that, now that the funeral bug might have caught my boyfriend. It could wear off, and I was sure it had for some people before, but helping others cope would appeal to Max, and now that he'd seen the transformation of a body from cold and dead to warm-looking and just sleeping, he might not be able to turn back.

"It was just so different."

"Well, you've played with numbers for your whole life, of course this is different."

He rolled his head toward me with a smile. "Yeah, speaking of that, I think I should probably go pick up my stuff from the hardware store. I'm pretty sure I'm not going to be needing that office space anymore. And if they want to rent it out to someone else, or if they're selling the place, it would be better if I were already out."

I hugged his arm. "Brilliant idea. Let's go."

"I don't know if I'd say it was brilliant."

"No, it is. It really is." I gave him the rundown on everything I'd found recently. This was the perfect excuse to go in to the hardware store without having to fake buying paint or another new toilet seat.

"Are you ready to go now?"

"I am. Let's go figure this out."

Chapter Twenty-three

The front door of the store was locked, but I could see lights on inside. I dragged Max around back and found that door open. I took it as an invitation and walked in like I owned the place. Because no one knew who would really own the place in the end, I figured I was as good as anyone else at the moment.

"Do you have your key?" I asked Max, who trailed right along behind me.

"I do, but are you sure we should be in here? I have a feeling they didn't leave the door open as an invitation."

"I'm choosing to take it that way anyway."

We walked across the concrete floor and up the metal stairs. I heard voices in the room where Hoagie had kept his base of operations. Could that be where the safe was? It was right next to the room Max rented. I was as quiet as possible on the metal walkway. No need to alert anyone. My grams hadn't been wrong when she said the best always listened in for information.

"I just don't get why you are doing all this. Call it done and let's go." It was a woman's voice, and one I didn't recognize.

"Because you were the one who got us into this mess. Now I have to figure out how to get us out. I don't know why she called you, and I still don't understand why you thought it would be a good idea to tell her she could sell the place to us, but I have to find that documentation or we might end up in jail, just like Uncle Maurice." That was a man's voice, deep and full of anger.

Uncle Maurice? As in Maurice Howard aka Hoagie? Oh my word. A nephew and niece of Hoagie? The ones he'd left behind and run away from when he'd testified against his twin brother?

"You're whining, and you have nothing to whine over. She said everything was in the works and there was no need to worry about anything. Yet here you are, being a worrier," the woman said.

"I have to worry for both of us because you don't seem to be smart enough to worry for yourself. Did you at least close the door out back when you came in from the car?"

Crap! I darted my eyes to Max. He quickly fumbled his office keys out of his pocket and unlocked the door directly behind him. We slipped in just as I heard the other door open and slam closed. We left the door cracked just a bit to see if she would say anything else on her way downstairs.

"Stupid bonehead. He messed it all up, and Wanda was going to hand it to him on a platter. Now it's all over the place, and he's not going to be smart enough to fix it, is he? No, he's not." She tromped down the stairs and, I assumed, went to the back door to pull it closed and maybe lock it. At least we'd be able to get out after they left. Whenever that was.

Turning to the room behind us, I wondered how long they'd stay and what it meant that they were here, whoever they were. Related to Hoagie yes, but how and who did they mean by "she" when they referenced "her" calling?

My eyes adjusted to the dimness of the room because we couldn't turn a light on without risking them seeing it under the door. Max shrugged when I turned to him. I shrugged back, not sure what to do but not wanting to make a single sound.

I did "eep" when I saw the window on the far wall was open just a bit and there were fingers curled around the windowsill.

I pointed, and Max took a step back when he looked.

Grabbing my phone out of the back pocket of my jeans, I texted Burton, because this wasn't something I could handle on my own, even with the awesome Max by my side.

"I'll lock the door," I whispered to Max. "You get ready to grab whoever that is before he or she decides to drop."

Once I quietly closed and locked the door, I crept to the window and threw up the sash. And what to my wandering eyes should appear but a very sweaty Hoagie, hanging on for dear life off the side of a two-story building.

His eyes were incredibly wide and his mouth open like a gaping fish on a hook. Max grabbed the older man's wrists before another second passed and yanked Hoagie up and into the room. He caught him before he hit the floor so as not to alert the people next door, who had gone back to fighting now that the back door was presumably locked.

"Hoagie," I whispered. More like breathed, because I wasn't sure what could be heard, though the two next door had reached a crescendo of screaming words that I didn't even understand at this point.

"Let me go."

"I can't do that. We need answers, and I'm pretty sure you're the only one who can provide them."

His eyes darted around the room. Looking for something to hit me with so he could get away? An escape route I wasn't aware of or couldn't see?

"Then we need to get out of here. Before they see us. Like now. I'll tell you anything you want to know. Just get me out of here before they come in and find the safe."

The safe! "Where is it?"

"I'm not telling you, and I can't get to it without making noise. We'll have to come back later."

"But will you be here later?" I looked him over to watch for anything that would tell me he was lying.

"Yes, I promise. I'm tired of running."

"Okay. I texted Burton and he should be here right about now." As if on cue, there was banging on the front door and shouts to open up.

Something clanged to the floor in the next room, and

footsteps scurried left and right. The two people clattered down the stairs and, I assumed, ran for the back, but from the yells to get down, I assumed the other half of the force was back there waiting for them.

Good work, boys.

And now I was left with a very tired-looking Hoagie with no smile in sight. His hair was standing up from his head and his eyes looked hollow.

"Where have you been?" I asked.

He gestured over to the cot in the corner. "Never thought I'd have to do this again. But I'd do it over and over if it would protect my kids. Nothing I wouldn't do to protect those ungrateful little buggers, no matter what they think of me."

Would he kill for them, though? Hopefully, we'd know soon.

But first, we had to get out of there. I had only told Burton that there were two intruders that I had watched walk into the store, not that there was anything else. And it was possible that because they'd caught those two, he wouldn't come in to check anything else.

As always, though, I shouldn't have thought of him if I didn't want him to appear out of nowhere.

"Tallie. I should have known."

"Oh, Burton, you're going to love this one. Or at least I think you will, once I figure out exactly what's going on here."

We all sat down in the break room at the hardware store. I'd asked Burton to give us a chance to get the story from Hoagie without going to the police station just yet. I thought it might be a good idea to let the others process the two intruders before bringing Hoagie into the mix, and he'd agreed. Apparently, the two people who had been trying to ransack the room next door were his niece and nephew. Family, at least in Hoagie's case, were people you couldn't trust. You couldn't run from them forever either, apparently.

See, good things do happen.

Hoagie brought me a cup of plain old coffee from the percolator on the desk next to his computer. I had to use powdered creamer and sugar packets galore, but it would suffice for the moment.

Burton and Max had opted for water, and once I took a sip of the coffee I almost wished I had gone for the same thing.

"So, let's hear it, Hoagie." Burton took out his trusty notepad and flipped to a new page.

"First I'd like to know what you know," the older man answered.

"No, it's not going to work like that." Burton crossed a foot over his knee and sat back in a folding chair, much like the one from bingo so many days ago. "I want to hear what you have to say. I'll protect your identity and I'll even give you a pass on hiding out in here when we've been looking everywhere for you, but I have to know what's going on, and I want it all from the horse's mouth."

Hoagie sighed and wiggled around in his chair, which he'd turned around to face our little circle. Max sat next to me on his folding chair with his water bottle dangling from his fingertips between his knees.

"In a state far, far away . . ." Hoagie laughed softly, but no one else even cracked a smile. "Okay, forty years ago in West Virginia, my twin brother murdered a man and I was given immunity for my part in gambling, racketeering and other nefarious activities if I testified against him."

I sat back stunned. I knew there was more to the story, but even this part was almost more than I thought I could handle hearing it directly from him, confirming what I hadn't wanted to believe in the first place.

"You were into all that stuff too?" I asked, unable to stop myself.

"I haven't always been a nice guy, Tallie, and I'm sure you've talked to my kids, which is par for your course, so you must know that I was also a harsh dad. But I wanted to protect them. Well, first I wanted to provide for them the only way I knew how, but then, when that fell through, I just wanted to protect them. You don't know what it's like to have to look over your shoulder every day, make sure no one ever takes a picture of you that could leave you recognizable, and don't get me started on this dang internet thing. Anybody could see anything at any time. I couldn't allow anyone to find us or they might have killed us. I have grandchildren to worry about."

"So you killed Ronda after you found out your brother had died, went down to take his body from the funeral home and tried to fake your own death by fire. Did you set that one?" Burton's voice was low, but you could hear the anger under the tone.

Hoagie shook his head. "I did none of those things.

Okay, I did some of them. But I did not kill my wife. I loved her, no matter how much people around here can't believe that. She used to be happy and vivacious. She loved all the money I made and the many things I could buy her. She loved being married to someone who could take care of her. And she never forgave me for moving her away from everyone she knew to this "Podunk town," in her words." He rearranged himself again in his chair and took a stapler off the desk to open and close it.

I was a little concerned about how he could use that stapler as a weapon if he chose to do so, but Burton just kept his eyes on the man and waited for more.

"She was angry and bitter that we had to live on the money a hardware store could make. But it was the only thing I knew how to do outside of the gambling and racketeering, and once I got in here, I actually enjoyed it. I came in under your father, Burton, and I saw that there might be another life for me if I'd take the chance. Ronda didn't see it that way and made me pay for it every day of my life."

"So you killed her. Which would make sense if she finally did something that tossed you over the edge and pushed you too far." I interjected the comment just in case I could throw him off guard. This was no longer the beloved uncle who threw Halloween parades and dressed up like Santa. This was a man who'd done awful things and gotten away with it just because he'd turned snitch.

"You've got it all wrong. I took everything she handed out and just cherished the fact that she was alive. She was the first one they'd threatened to kill, along with the two kids we had at the time. They were going to leave me until last so that I could suffer through each of their deaths. I couldn't do it. I couldn't stay there and watch them be hurt, so I took the deal the government gave me and chose to move us out and start a new life."

"And you lived that way for forty years. What changed?" Burton flipped to the next page, keeping an avid eye on Hoagie. I had started looking at the floorboards to see if I could find the outline of a safe. With whatever info he'd brought with him from the past, we might be able to confirm or discredit his story. I was on board with either one at this point.

Hoagie sighed, and it ruffled my bangs. "Ronda must have kept tabs on her family and mine throughout the years. And like I said, that damn internet. She saw when Jerry got out of jail and called her sister to congratulate her."

"Wait, her sister was married to your brother?" The story just kept getting stranger and stranger.

"Yes. We met Wanda and Wendy at the same time. Ronda was Wendy before we left."

"So, your wife calls her sister to congratulate her on getting her husband back after forty years and then what happens?" Burton asked.

"Well, a lot at once. See, the government gave the deal to the wrong brother. I was the one who committed most of the crimes and Wanda knew it. She demanded that Ronda give her something for everything she had lost and Ronda saw a way to keep me from gifting the store to Nathan. She signed it over to Wanda's son."

"Can she do that, though?" Max asked. "She'd need your signature too."

"Which she got when she threatened to go back to West Virginia and lead each and every one of them here if I didn't give in to her demands. She thought that with Jerry dead, we'd be able to go back to our old lives."

"And when was this?" Burton's pencil was poised over his notepad.

"Two days before Christmas. I wasn't happy, but I couldn't think of what else to do. I had promised Nathan the store, so instead, I told him I'd give him a big raise and a promotion to store manager before I handed the store over to my nephew."

"And then you'd just what? Retire? Because as far as I can tell, it sounds like even with your brother dead, you'd still be in danger." Burton had a valid point and I was very interested to hear what Hoagie would say.

"We would have been, no matter what she thought, but she wouldn't listen. So, I figured Ronda and I would fake our deaths on a deserted road and run away to start over somewhere she wanted to be, with a life she wanted to lead. It was the least I could do for her after all I'd put her through over the years. But then she was killed, and it all fell apart. I want that person's soul in my hands and their neck under my foot." He snapped the stapler open and closed and his breathing got harsher. I scooted my chair back, then waited to see what Burton would do.

"Good story, Hoagie, but I'm not sure I believe it. I think you killed her to finally get away from her and then realized that you'd miscalculated when the fire you set to throw off investigators by pretending to be the firebug didn't jump across to your building. Were you going to let the thing burn down so no one got it?"

He shrugged his shoulders, raised his hands as if to show he didn't know and said, "That was the plan." Then he chucked the stapler at Burton's head and made a run for it.

Chapter Twenty-four

Hoagie had dinged Burton in the temple, so Max ran out of the room to hunt him down while I tried to get Burton to respond. He finally did wince and groan, so I felt he was going to live, thankfully. I took the radio out of his belt and pushed down the button to ask anyone who was in the area for help. Matt answered back that he'd be right there.

I heard pounding footsteps and some grunting but stayed with Burton because I didn't need to see what was going on. I believed Max had it handled. Or at least I hoped so.

And my hopes were very much confirmed when Max yelled, "Got him!"

I chanced a glance over the metal railing on the walkway, and there was Hoagie, strapped to a toilet with one of those winches people used to hold down luggage on the roof of their car.

"Nicely done." I said.

"All part of the service, ma'am," he answered, and this time I laughed.

Burton groaned again behind me, and I turned to help him sit up.

"Did you get him?"

"Max did. He has him downstairs, ready to be taken away. I have a feeling that might be the last we get from him, because he's going to lawyer up immediately."

"Maybe not." Burton removed a key from the floor next to where his nose had been. "I picked up the stapler and found that there was a small compartment for that key in the bottom."

"Your dad says there's a safe in here somewhere."

"Does he, now?"

"He also said you're very good at your job and he misses you." Okay, that last part was a lie, but it was Christmastime, a time for miracles, and maybe Burton wouldn't be so grumpy if he had his dad back in his life.

"Yeah, thanks. Now pull the other leg, Tallie; I like them to match."

I harrumphed. "Fine, but he was very lonely, and I guess he doesn't get many visitors, and he feels cooped up. I just thought if you could maybe go over and tell him what ends up happening here, maybe you could smooth things over. He's not getting any younger. I'll even give you the snickerdoodles I told him I'd deliver to him. That should make the road like polished steel. And he did say you do a good job."

"I'll think about it. First, let's find the safe."

We hunted for about ten minutes before I was able to find a springy board in the floor. I was a pro after finding all the flaws in the third floor before we hired a contractor, so I knew my way around.

Pushing on the nails, they both sank down, and then the boards creaked open and there was the safe.

Burton put in the key and turned it. I don't know what Burton thought we'd find. Heck, I didn't know what I thought we would find, but I highly doubt either of us considered the fact that there might be bundles and bundles and bundles of wrapped one-hundred-dollar bills.

"Quite the haul."

"Quite the savings," I said instead. "Why wouldn't he have given some of this to Ronda to make her happier? I'm just not sure I believe he didn't kill her."

"Me neither, but I need evidence. I need his prints on the can, although they're going to be there anyway because he put the dang thing on the shelf. I would need to know where he purchased it, but I already know where it came from, and who had access to it is not a mystery. All I don't know is how he did it and why now." Burton ruffled through the stacks of money to see if there was anything else there.

"I think the why is that he wanted out, saw a way and blamed Ronda for taking away the comfortable life he'd made for himself."

"It's a fine theory, Tallie, and one I'm surprised you thought of. I was sure you'd see through everything and zero in on me, seeing as how everyone thinks you're the smartest person in town. Maybe not so much if you didn't see what was right under your nose," Nathan said from the door with a gun in his hand.

Really? No way was it Nathan. No way!

The gun shook a little in his hands, and the smile looked forced. I stared at him, knowing he'd never actually use the thing. Well, scratch that. He might use it if he was pressed, but I doubted he wanted to.

I knew who had killed Ronda now; I just needed to figure out how to get an admission from the right person.

"Ah, now I see it, Nathan. It was you the whole time, wasn't it?" I willed Burton to go along with me. Sometimes it worked with Max, or my mom, but I wasn't sure Burton would get my drift. "You killed Ronda outside the bingo hall, and then, when Hoagie found out, he agreed to hide it for you and disappear so that you wouldn't get into trouble. After all, you've helped him for so many years, and Ronda wanted to cut you out of getting the store. With her gone, he could disappear too, like he had forty years ago, and start off fresh somewhere else. Burton here could just assume that Hoagie had gotten away, and eventually, it would be a cold case."

"Right." Nathan looked back and forth between me and Burton. His hand shook some more, and I wondered how long he'd be able to keep the gun up.

"I mean, Ronda was awful to you, wasn't she? When she found out Hoagie's brother had died, she wanted to give the store to her nephew, not a thankless kid who'd never done anything for her and who she treated like a piece of garbage any chance she got. Am I right?"

He shook his head and folded his lips in on themselves. But he said, "Right," again.

"And I'm sure all those times she snubbed you and never invited you to do anything with the family were just knives in your back over and over again. Like you were being cut out of something that had finally been good in your life, or at least you thought it would be good until you met up with that evil lady. Hoagie was so good and then his wife was a piece of—"

"Stop! Just stop!" The hand holding the gun wavered some more and then dropped to his side. "Just stop." This time it was said more quietly, and tears ran down his cheeks. "She was never like that to me. She might not always have been the nicest of people, but she was decent, and in her own way she loved me. Heck, she was nicer to me than she was to her own kids most days. I did everything for her and she appreciated it. She even remembered my birthday every year and brought me the kind of cake I liked when Jenna forgot."

"And Jenna wasn't a big fan of the idea of you not getting the store outright. She wanted that handed to you, so she could be the owner's wife and not have to work anymore unless she wanted to," I said softly as Max came up behind Nathan and took the gun out of his hand.

"Yes," he whispered.

"And Jenna was tired of being snubbed and not getting her due because Ronda had wanted you to marry someone better. In fact, she had thought you'd marry Chrissy and you'd all be one big family. She liked you that much. But then Chrissy thwarted her plan and you married Jenna within months. Jenna, who always felt second-best. Jenna, who can be supernice as long as she's getting what she wants, but watch out if she is crossed."

"Yes."

"That's enough, Tallie," Burton said. He stood next to Nathan and put a hand on his shoulder. "Son, I'm going to have to take you in for questioning, but we'll get this sorted out. As far as things go, you're not in too much trouble, but I'm going to need you to be honest with us. First, though, I need you to tell me where your wife is."

"She's downstairs in the car, waiting for me to come out with all the money she saw in the floor one time when she was visiting me for lunch. She wanted everything. And when Hoagie had to tell us that the store was being given to a relative, he promised things would work out okay. He said he'd make sure I was paid handsomely, if he had to make up the difference himself. I told him it wasn't necessary, that I was willing to work for an honest wage, but Jenna wasn't having any of it. She told me that she'd hit Ronda with the can that night because the woman had told her she hated her. That when she saw Jenna keying her car, Ronda yelled at her to jump off a bridge and make my life easier for one minute. Jenna grabbed a can of varnish from out of the back seat of the car and hit her hard in the head."

"And when you found out, you told Hoagie, who had already made plans to disappear because he didn't want his sister-in-law to find them," Burton offered. "And he knew just where to find a body that could double as his in a fire that investigators would think the firebug set. And because Ronda was killed before the will could be changed, the store would still be yours outright."

"Yes."

Bingo.

"Did you really know or were you guessing?" Burton asked as I sat across from him in his office. Hoagie was seated in the chair next to me and Nathan was down the hall in a room with Jenna for the time being. He'd been given a chance to convince her to tell the truth. I didn't think she'd actually take it, but I was very thankful that Burton had given it to him.

"The pieces were all there. She was angry that night at bingo and she kept dropping hints that she would be in the midst of a life change coming up soon and wouldn't need my job anymore. Hoagie was the kind of person who would do anything he could to protect his children—he said so himself—and Nathan was just like one of his."

"She's right," Hoagie said. "I didn't want to get into all of this, but I knew if Jenna went to jail for murder, Nathan was going to be hurt, and I just couldn't see doing that to him, not if there was an easy fix. I knew how to vanish, and I thought I might be able to do it again and save everyone the trouble of finding out what had really happened."

"So what will you do now?" Burton twirled his pen around his fingers like a baton majorette.

"Well, with the body back at the right funeral home and my wife gone, I guess I could start again anywhere." He shrugged. "I liked it here, but maybe it's time for me to go."

"Or you could tell your children that you're not really dead and live the rest of your life with them and helping out Nathan. He really seemed lost without you when he was running the store alone. It's possible that without Jenna around to demand things, he'd be happy to stay in the status quo."

Getting up to pace, Hoagie did two turns around the room. "I did have an offer from a big box store that I could entertain. I'd give the kids their inheritance and Nathan and I could start a woodworking shop. The boy is a whiz with furniture, and without the noose of the store, we'd be able to do whatever we wanted. No one knows about all that cash except you guys, and the kids would think they'd gotten so much more because they'd expected to get nothing at all."

"I like it." I grabbed his hand. "And I'll put in the first order for a new chest of drawers for my walk-in closet."

Hoagie laughed, then Burton walked him out to the front.

I took a pen from Burton's cup on his desk and tried to get it to flip end over end on my fingers, but I was too clumsy.

"It takes practice," he said when I groaned and threw the thing back into the cup.

"Yeah, well, that's not a priority right now. I'm just happy the killer is caught and going to jail."

"Now, if you could just hand me the arsonist on a platter to ring in the New Year, I'd be a happy man."

I touched the side of my nose. "I'm working on something even as we speak."

I knew I wasn't actually working on anything, but I did have an idea. When I got home, I went back through the paperwork Sherman had given me and then called Hoagie. "You have a minute? I'd like to see if you can get me some prices."

"Sure, come on over. And anything you want is free at this point. I can't thank you enough."

"I have to make a stop first, but I'll be there soon."

I said goodbye to Max and hustled out the door and down the street. I had a theory, and this one was sounder than the last was. All I had to do was figure out if it was actually true. I was pretty sure I knew who the arsonist

was. The kid in the hoodie. Was I sure Zeke was the cul-
prit, and could I prove it?

"Here are those cookies I promised you." I handed
over the plate of snickerdoodles with a flourish when Hal
Burton came into the foyer of the retirement home on
Keller.

"But my son called to say he was bringing them by
this evening."

"Oh, did he?" I smiled cheekily. "I guess I forgot."

One corner of his mouth lifted. "I'm sure you did."

"Oh, yes, that's me, so forgetful. I hope he'll deliver
them with a smile on his face."

"Well," he said gruffly. "Maybe not a smile, but he did
hang up chuckling when I told him about trying to get
one over on you."

I could let that pass. The orderly from my first visit
came by with a glass of water and avoided all eye contact
with me. But I smelled the strong odor of paint thinner
again and recognized him from Bertie's cleanup crew this
time. He was the one who'd given me the sullen look.
Things were clicking into place. And now that I looked
harder at him, he was also the one I'd had a brief glance
at as he walked quickly from the Clemenses' house with
his earbuds in and his hoodie on, as if just out for a stroll.

My blood began to sing, but I tried as hard as I could
to be calm and cool. "So, do you want to do a little
sleuthing for me? Now that you almost got one over on
me, how about we get one over on your son? He'll be
floored."

Hal's chuckle had a maniacal edge, and I hoped I
hadn't made the wrong decision by letting him in on my
mission.

He led me up the stairs to the live-in quarters for the

staff and then guarded the door while I stepped into the orderly's room. Under his bed, I found nothing, and in the closet, nothing again. He had to keep his supply somewhere. If he'd bought a can from Hoagie every single time he used one, Hoagie would have noticed, or at least made a note of it.

So where did he keep it, and how did he get it?

I went back out of the hallway shaking my head, then glanced out the window and noticed the kid walking to the back shed, looking all around him as if making sure he wasn't being watched.

He opened the old, warped wooden door and stared inside before stepping in quickly and pulling the door shut. Because the latch was on the outside he couldn't close it all the way or he would risk locking himself in.

And that was precisely what I was hoping for. I watched in fascination as the ruddy glow of a lit cigarette lighter peeked out through the crack in the door.

I called Burton, let him give me his usual greeting and then told him to come on over to the retirement home to pick up his arsonist in the act.

He was there in a flash. I guess I had forgotten to tell him that the arsonist wasn't actually setting the place on fire, only flicking his lighter, and his father was in no danger. Whoops.

Oh well; everything was fine in the end. And when I went to check on Hoagie making up with his family, they were laughing for the first time in a long time.

Walking back to my penthouse above the dead, I looked forward to spending time with Max in the last few hours before they dropped the wrench downtown. Sherman would pull out his biggest fire truck and the town would hook up the eight-foot wrench. As the final countdown of the year began, they'd slowly winch down the wrench.

Hey, at least we didn't live in the next town over, where they dropped a pickle. Or the one across the river, where they dropped a bologna. Nope, we just had a wrench, and when it hit the ground, I'd kiss Max and start a whole new year with a bunch of changes in store. But between the two of us, we'd manage it.

And you know how I knew?

Max flipped the light on upstairs and waved at me from the bay window. Mr. Fleefers was on one side, bathing himself, and Peanut had her paws up on the windowsill. I could hear her barking from across the street, the big rascal.

I laughed and laughed. Right there was my world and I knew it.

Grab These Cozy Mysteries
from
Kensington Books

Follow P.I. Savannah Reid
with
G.A. McKevett

Romantic Suspense from
Lisa Jackson

Absolute Fear	0-8217-7936-2	$7.99US/$9.99CAN
Afraid to Die	1-4201-1850-1	$7.99US/$9.99CAN
Almost Dead	0-8217-7579-0	$7.99US/$10.99CAN
Born to Die	1-4201-0278-8	$7.99US/$9.99CAN
Chosen to Die	1-4201-0277-X	$7.99US/$10.99CAN
Cold Blooded	1-4201-2581-8	$7.99US/$8.99CAN
Deep Freeze	0-8217-7296-1	$7.99US/$10.99CAN
Devious	1-4201-0275-3	$7.99US/$9.99CAN
Fatal Burn	0-8217-7577-4	$7.99US/$10.99CAN
Final Scream	0-8217-7712-2	$7.99US/$10.99CAN
Hot Blooded	1-4201-0678-3	$7.99US/$9.49CAN
If She Only Knew	1-4201-3241-5	$7.99US/$9.99CAN
Left to Die	1-4201-0276-1	$7.99US/$10.99CAN
Lost Souls	0-8217-7938-9	$7.99US/$10.99CAN
Malice	0-8217-7940-0	$7.99US/$10.99CAN
The Morning After	1-4201-3370-5	$7.99US/$9.99CAN
The Night Before	1-4201-3371-3	$7.99US/$9.99CAN
Ready to Die	1-4201-1851-X	$7.99US/$9.99CAN
Running Scared	1-4201-0182-X	$7.99US/$10.99CAN
See How She Dies	1-4201-2584-2	$7.99US/$8.99CAN
Shiver	0-8217-7578-2	$7.99US/$10.99CAN
Tell Me	1-4201-1854-4	$7.99US/$9.99CAN
Twice Kissed	0-8217-7944-3	$7.99US/$9.99CAN
Unspoken	1-4201-0093-9	$7.99US/$9.99CAN
Whispers	1-4201-5158-4	$7.99US/$9.99CAN
Wicked Game	1-4201-0338-5	$7.99US/$9.99CAN
Wicked Lies	1-4201-0339-3	$7.99US/$9.99CAN
Without Mercy	1-4201-0274-5	$7.99US/$10.99CAN
You Don't Want to Know	1-4201-1853-6	$7.99US/$9.99CAN

Available Wherever Books Are Sold!
Visit our website at **www.kensingtonbooks.com**